# BAREFOOT DOGS

STORIES

## ANTONIO RUIZ-CAMACHO

SCRIBNER

New York   London   Toronto   Sydney   New Delhi

SCRIBNER
A Division of Simon & Schuster, Inc.
1230 Avenue of the Americas
New York, NY 10020

First Scribner hardcover edition March 2015

SCRIBNER and design are registered trademarks of The Gale Group, Inc., used under license by Simon & Schuster, Inc., the publisher of this work.

For information about special discounts for bulk purchases, please contact Simon & Schuster Special Sales at 1-866-506-1949 or business@simonandschuster.com.

The Simon & Schuster Speakers Bureau can bring authors to your live event. For more information or to book an event, contact the Simon & Schuster Speakers Bureau at 1-866-248-3049 or visit our website at www.simonspeakers.com.

Interior design by Erich Hobbing

Manufactured in the United States of America

1   3   5   7   9   10   8   6   4   2

Library of Congress Cataloging-in-Publication Data is available.

ISBN 978-1-4767-8496-0
ISBN 978-1-4767-8498-4 (ebook)

For Valentina

For Emiliano and Guillermo

# CONTENTS

It Will Be Awesome Before Spring                                    1

Okie                                                                15

Origami Prunes                                                      29

I Clench My Hands into Fists and They Look Like
   Someone Else's                                    53

Deers                                                               71

Better Latitude                                                     87

Her Odor First                                                     109

Barefoot Dogs                                                      115

The Arteaga Family Tree                                            139

Acknowledgments                                                    143

Our textbooks confirmed this:
Mexico, as can be seen on the map,
is shaped like a cornucopia, a horn of plenty . . .
A future of plenitude and universal well-being was predicted,
without specifying just how it would be achieved.
Clean cities without injustice, poor people, violence, congestion, or garbage.
Every family with an ultramodern and aerodynamic (words from that era) house.
No one will want for anything.
Machines will do all the work.
Streets full of trees and fountains,
traveled by silent, nonpolluting vehicles that never collide.
Paradise on earth.
Finally, utopia will have been found.
—José Emilio Pacheco, *Battles in the Desert*

# BAREFOOT DOGS

# IT WILL BE AWESOME BEFORE SPRING

It is the year everybody's planning to spend the summer in Italy. Tammy and Sash will take a photography workshop in Florence and Jen will take a cruise around the Mediterranean with her family, and mine will rent a house in Tuscany. We've already made arrangements to meet in Milan for a couple of days and perhaps drive to Portofino and hang out there for another day or two—Italian highways are the best, we've heard, and no one cares about speed limits there, same as here, but highways there don't suck, so everybody agrees it will be awesome. Before spring breaks, we're already taking Italian conversation over cappuccinos at Klein's on Avenida Masaryk once a week with this beautiful middle-aged Genovese woman I remember as Giovanna but I'm sure that was not her name. She looks like Diane von Furstenberg when she was in her prime, only with much less expensive clothes. She wound up in Mexico because she met some guy in Cancún, and has been trying to make a living here since, teaching Italian and any other language to foreign executives, because she's a polyglot. Whenever we want a break from class we ask her to tell us stories about her other students—she's an avid raconteur too, so she can talk and talk for hours on end—and she comes up with the wildest tales. My memories of that year have started to blur and I can only recall the story of the Danish executive who's taking English conversation and fashions a grinding, horrible accent, our teacher says, flapping her branchy hands over our cappuccino glasses as if they're logs on fire and she's trying to turn them into embers. Irregular nouns and verbs make this poor Danish lady crazy, Diane—let's call the Italian polyglot that—admits with a frown that makes the crisp features of her face look worn rather than sophisticated, so every time Diane asks her to talk about her morning routine, the Danish lady says, "Well, firrst ting rright out of my bet, I torouffly wash my teets."

It is the year there's only room for Italy in our minds, and so every Thursday evening after Italian conversation, we thunder into Mixup and sort through the World Music section, looking for CDs from Italian pop singers as if we're British schoolgirls and the Beatles' real names are Umberto Tozzi and Gianluca Grignani and Claudio Baglioni and Zucchero. We buy every Italian tune we can, from Lucio Dalla's number ones to the latest from Laura Pausini—we only buy her albums in Italian, though, and pretend to ignore the appalling fact that her songs in Spanish are as mainstream as Luis Miguel's—and spend long weekend hours at Sash's or Tammy's learning cheesy lyrics by heart, mastering our accents, dreaming of Milan. It is the year we check out all of Fellini from the university's library and watch *Il Postino* and *La Vita è Bella* and *Cinema Paradiso* so many times we can reenact scenes from those flicks on the sidewalks of Paseo de la Reforma at 4:00 a.m. after partying at Bulldog, where we dance on the tables, vodka tonics in hand, lip-synching to No Doubt's "It's My Life" or Outkast's "Hey Ya!" or Nirvana's classic "Smells Like Teen Spirit," thinking how cheap and tacky these songs are, how insignificant they sound compared to the subtle honeylike grandeur of Fiordaliso's "Non Voglio Mica la Luna."

It is the year we take internships in museums across the city because we dream of becoming artists after college. Sash and Tammy land gigs at Centro de la Imagen, and Jen at Museo de Arte Moderno, and I get the best of all, at Antiguo Colegio de San Ildefonso, helping to curate the first-ever solo exhibit of David Hockney in Mexico, which is beyond amazing and makes my three stupendous friends rattle with jealousy. I boast about my job even though all I do for those ten hours a week is mail invitations for the opening reception, organize large boxes of leaflets into brick-thick stacks, fax documents overseas, drag superheavy crates to storage—tedious and exhausting chores I've never had to do before, the novelty of which feels exciting and paramount. I feel like I'm carrying Hockney's posterity on my shoulders, like his success in Mexico depends on me. I get a taste of what the real city feels like, and I think it's not as bad as it looks from the outside.

It is the year I'm nineteen. It is the year life will change for us, but we don't know any of that yet.

It is the year we meet people that don't live in the same neighborhoods as us, Polanco, Lomas, Tecamachalco. It is the year we get to know real artists who rent studios in dangerous districts on the other side of the city, and it is the year we socialize with historians and anthropologists and performance artists and book editors who live paycheck to paycheck and don't have cars; these are fascinating, glamorous people who ride the subway and take taxicabs. It is a new and unexplored world within the same city we were born and have always lived, and every time we venture into it we feel as if we're crossing an invisible fence, trespassing into a forbidden side of ourselves: messier, wilder, sexier.

As we start mingling with the native people of that other city, we learn it is also the year everybody's talking about kidnappings; the wave of panic of the late nineties is back with a vengeance, they announce. They're all sharing the stories they've heard, gory details about what's happened to this or that friend the last time they grabbed a taxicab. At a party in an abandoned building behind the Metropolitan Cathedral, the associate curator of Viceregal Art at Museo de la Ciudad de México tells the fresh story of a dear friend of his: It's around nine o'clock at night and this woman, a young photographer who had just returned from the Sierra Tarahumara, where she'd been working on a multimedia project to premiere at Art Basel in Miami, catches a cab, a little green-and-white Beetle, on the corner of Álvaro Obregón and Frontera, and asks the driver to take her to Barracuda Bar, "The one by Parque España," she specifies. A friend of hers is celebrating his birthday there—actually, the very curator who's telling the story—she explains to the driver in a jolly mood. The guy pulls resolutely into the traffic and feigns interest in her conversation, but when they're only one block into the ride he halts at a stoplight and a couple of fat guys step into the taxicab and fill the minuscule space of the backseat on either side of her.

"My friend hasn't realized what's going on yet when these motherfuckers start beating the shit out of her," the curator says, "fists into her torso and her face as if softening a pillow, like when you're getting ready for a sweet night's sleep. Next they take her on a merry-go-round of ATMs," he explains, "forcing her to withdraw all the cash she can with a knife pinching her lower back, until she reaches the daily limit on the three cards she carries in her purse. The guy at the wheel says they need to wait until midnight to continue, and in the meantime they drive my friend around Colonia Roma and Colonia Doctores, just making time, listening to old ranchera music, whistling to the rusty tunes that pop from the speakers," the curator says. "Then one of the other guys drops something like, 'I'm fucking starving, aren't you guys?' and so they stop by a taco sudado stand to grab a bite. The hungry one takes everybody's order but my friend's," the curator says, "and out he goes to fetch the food while the other two stay inside, watching over her to make sure she doesn't escape. The hungry one comes back with a bunch of tacos wrapped in brown paper in one hand and three bottles of Coca-Cola dangling from the other," the curator says, and I can imagine the scene clearly, the sound of soda bottles clinking against each other unnervingly. "The driver pulls back into the traffic jam and the three motherfuckers have dinner while cruising streets," the curator continues, "these three pigs and my friend crammed into this little Beetle taxicab that reeks of damp taco and sweat of swine. They finish dinner but it isn't midnight yet, and they're growing bored. A couple minutes later one of them says something like, 'Hey, guys, we didn't have dessert! What if we all fuck this little cunt instead?' The three of them take a look at her, as if considering if she's worth the effort. 'Nah, she's not that hot,' the driver says, but they have nothing else to do until midnight, so in the end they all vote for the go," says the curator with a broken voice. He has to pause, he looks shaken, like he won't be able to continue the story, and everybody around him is silent looking at him with wide eyes, everybody thinking, This is a joke, right? and I feel weird because the story is so horrible it can't be true, but I realize that this is what living the real life of the city must be like, and this makes me feel grown up and wild and independent. I look at Jen and Tammy and Sash, who are listening as well, and I catch the confused signals on their faces, fascination, horror, and disbelief in their eyes.

"They drive off into what looks like Colonia Portales and they park somewhere on a lightless street," the curator finally says, "and they take turns and get her as dessert. At some point midnight arrives and they resume their pilgrimage to the ATMs, but my friend's credit and debit cards are maxed out in the first attempt, and rage overtakes them. 'You're fucking broke, bitch?' the driver yells at her." The curator says his friend doesn't reply because, at that point, she's realized that crying or begging won't make a difference. She wants to believe they have nothing else to take from her. "They pull up somewhere around Eje Central, and she seems to be right because they swing the taxicab door open and throw her onto the sidewalk. She's already lying on the ground when one of them steps out of the cab and pulls down the zipper of his pants and pisses all over her. She doesn't remember feeling anything at that moment," the curator says—everybody around him, including myself, is now looking at him with tears in our eyes—"she only gets to hear the other motherfuckers cracking up, howling in celebration inside the taxicab. The guy finishes, squats down by her side, and whispers in her ear, 'We're keeping your purse, muffin, so if we feel like visiting you one of these days we know where you live.' He gets back in the cab, and she watches from the corner of her eye as the little Beetle fades away. And here comes the worst part of the whole thing," the curator says. "A sense of glee she'd never experienced before takes over her when she sees them disappear into the night."

It is the year we realize we've never traveled by subway or taxicab. In Mexico, that is. We've ridden subways in places like Paris or New York, on vacations. I've taken taxicabs in London and Frankfurt and San Francisco, I say to Jen and Tammy and Sash while we listen to Jovanotti's CD *Il Quinto Mondo*, which is playing on Sash's Bose stereo. Tammy adds

6

that she took cabs and the subway in Tokyo with her parents two summers before, and taxicabs there are definitely best. Jen visited Japan the summer after graduating from high school and agrees with her. "I did both too. The Tokyo subway is very clean," she points out, "but the taxi drivers there wear gloves; they reminded me of the bellboys at The Plaza. So glam!" Sash intervenes to remind us that some subway stations in Paris smell like piss and sweat, and we all nod and exclaim, "Yeah!" with a tone that means yeah and yuck at the same time. She adds that she had a similar experience in Barcelona the previous summer. We look at each other and admit we're wondering whether the subway in Milan will be filthy too, and one part of my brain struggles to understand why subways in such nice cities have to smell bad, but then Jen says, "I don't even want to think what the subway here smells like!" and we all yell, "Ewwww!" and crack up really hard.

It is the end of the semester and we feel June approaching fast. We get antsy thinking we're not ready for Italy. Summer's in peril, but Diane tells us there's nothing to worry about, we've made such great progress in recent weeks, we'll do great (If you already speak Spanish and French, Italian is a piece of cake, we all agree that evening before Diane arrives, but we refrain from sharing this with her because we don't want to hurt her feelings). We're discussing the Larousse book of coniugazione that Diane suggested we buy when Tammy asks her if she's ever ridden the subway in Mexico City. Diane looks at her in disbelief. Then she replies, "Ma che domanda è questa?" and I explain we've noticed that everybody's talking about kidnappings, and we wonder whether she's afraid to live in the city now. Diane pauses for a moment, as if giving serious consideration to Tammy's question, and then replies that she doesn't know whether she's afraid or not, but she couldn't live elsewhere now because Mexico is the place where she found the love of her life.

A few weeks pass and it is one of our last Italian conversation classes before summer starts. It is late May and daily thunderstorms will soon overtake the city. Next week, we'll have a graduation dinner at La Cosa Nostra and Diane says she'll miss us all but has no doubt we'll have the best Italian summer ever. The class is drawing to a close when she asks whether one of us could do a big favor for her. "I am a bit embarrassed to ask for this, but I think you'll understand," she says. She grows soft and frail, the features of her astounding visage crumple, like a puppy's begging for forgiveness. "You can ask for anything, Diane!" we reassure her in both Italian and Spanish, cheering with anticipation. I wonder whether this means we'll get to know more about Diane's private life at last, and the mysterious lover for whom she left her life in Italy behind. I wonder why she insists on keeping his identity from us, and sometimes I wonder even whether he really exists. With so many metropolises she could live in, why would she choose Mexico City? She was living in the very Milan when she met this guy! Diane sighs in relief and tells us that her mamma lives in Genova—she actually called her *madre*, but it sounded so Spanish, so ordinary, that I prefer to remember her saying *mamma* instead—and she hasn't seen her since she moved to Mexico three years ago, and as much as she'd like to visit her, she doesn't think that it will be possible in the near future. "Lezioni di conversazione don't make people rich," she says, as if admitting for the first time that her life is not as glamorous as it looks from the outside.

Diane's mamma worked as an executive assistant for the Municipalità Genovese for forty years and is now retired; she lives alone in the tiny flat on via della Maddalena where

Diane's family has always lived, in the historic heart of the city, close to the piers. Diane's mamma is a widow, the polyglot's dad died ten years ago, leaving the two of them with no one to look after them but each other. "I am an only child, too!" Jen reveals, and Diane makes an effort to receive Jen's comment with enthusiasm, but I can tell she prefers to go on with the details of her own story. Diane's mamma gets a retirement check from the Italian government every month, but recently she's been struggling to make ends meet. The euro has raised the cost of living to the skies and she could use some extra help, but MoneyGram and FedEx are so pricey they're not really an option for Diane. So now that her favorite students are traveling to Italy, Diane was wondering, wouldn't it be great if she could put together a suitcase with new clothes and shoes and even some facial creams and over-the-counter medicines for her mamma, along with some cash, and wouldn't it be fantastic if one of us could deliver all that to her in Genova?

"I'd be forever grateful," she says in a voice so low that the words greet the evening air in a whisper. "We all could go visit your mom!" Tammy exclaims right away. "It'd be great to meet her!" Jen adds. "We could even take her out to dinner and practice conversazione on her!" Sash offers, making the idea sound immediately like The Truest Italian Summer Experience Ever. I volunteer to carry the bag, and we decide we'll iron out the details of our expedition to Genova over chianti the following week. "Molto grazie, i miei amori!" Diane exclaims, back to her original marvelous self again. She refuses to let us pay for the cappuccinos that night. I'm excited to meet Diane's mamma and venture into her past, but I'm shocked to learn she doesn't have the resources I'd assumed she had from looking at the fierce features of her face, the exclusive shape of her body, the European self-confidence she carries herself with around Mexicans.

In the evening we bypass Mixup and head directly to Tammy's, where we discuss Diane's petition with curiosity and fascination while listening to *La Traviata*. Italy has never been closer, the summer of our lives has already started. I get home later than usual, dying to tell my parents about Diane's mamma, but they are not there (Nicolasa, my younger sister, is not at home either; she's in Costa Rica on an end-of-school-year trip with her class).

Justina, our nanny, who has taken care of us since we were born, is waiting for me in the kitchen. The small TV set where she likes to watch soap operas while cooking dinner is off, which immediately raises a red flag. Justina is past forty-five, but her round, bright face remains girlish as ever. Tonight she looks exhausted, as if a decade has run her over since the last time I saw her, that morning. Her eyes are swollen, redder than usual.

"Are you okay?" I ask, kissing her on each cheek—my superb friends and I have been practicing kissing like Italians do, and I practice with Justina as well—and this makes her smile wearily, but instead of answering she asks whether I've already had dinner. I say I have, but she insists.

"Fercita, are you sure you don't want me to prepare a sandwich or some quesadillas for you?" she asks imploringly, as if by saying yes I'd save her life.

I say I'm sure and press her further, for something's definitely going on. Justina coaxes me into the living room. She says we need to talk. When we sit on the sofa, Justina says Mom and Dad are not home because they're at Grandpa's. He left his office yesterday to head out for lunch and didn't return. He didn't go home either. He hasn't called. They've tried to reach him on his cell phone, but he's not answering. Mom and Dad and my uncles and my aunts are at his home, waiting for news. I struggle to understand why this is all a big deal, Grandpa should be somewhere fun, hanging around with his friends, probably partying hard, he won't call his children to tell them that, right? It makes no sense for Justina, and everybody else, to freak out.

Then it hits me.

This image of Grandpa taking a taxicab outside his office and disappearing into the city thunders into my head, but it makes no sense, I say to myself. Grandpa doesn't need to take taxicabs. He never takes one—here. These things only happen to people who don't have cars. These things don't happen to people who live in Polanco, people like us, like Grandpa.

"I'm sure he's fine," I say, but I say it more to myself than to Justina. "I'm heading to Grandpa's to tell Mom and Dad there's nothing to worry about."

"No!" Justina raises her voice. "Your parents asked me not to let you go there, they think it's better if you wait here, Fernanda."

"Then I'm going to call them and see what's up!" I cry, and it surprises me to hear my own voice, cracking. "I need to talk to them, Jus!"

"No, don't do that, please!" Justina's voice is higher than mine now, and as out of control. "They need to keep the phone lines open at all times, in case Don Victoriano or someone else calls with information. They said they'd call as soon as they can."

I don't know what else to say. As I head to my room I feel my brain getting stuffed, turning heavy. I call Sash and Tammy and Jen from my cell phone, but I only reach Tammy. I tell her I need to see her because something's happened.

"What is it, cara mia?" she asks, but I can't say it on the phone. Actually I can hardly speak. I try to remember the last time I saw Grandpa, and I can't. Instead, I see him in the back of a taxicab, sandwiched between a couple guys with black balaclavas covering their faces, knives pressed against his ribs. "Okay, don't worry, Fer. Let's meet at Klein's," Tammy says. "I'll try to get there as soon as possible. I'll text Sash and Jen and ask them to reach us there. Ciao, bella."

I'm the first to arrive. I don't know what to do with my hands, with my purse. I call the waiter and ask him to bring me a pack of Marlboros from the tobacco stand next door. I hate smoking, it makes me sick, but tonight I need it. In my head, Grandpa keeps asking the fat guys with balaclavas to calm down, everything can be worked out. I close my eyes and try to force myself to picture Grandpa somewhere else. I try to imagine him at a nightclub in Centro Histórico, going wild, I try to imagine him heading out to Acapulco with his friends for a crazy last-minute sugar daddies' getaway, but nothing works, the image of him in the taxicab's stuck in my head.

It is the year all the members of my family will end up fleeing Mexico, following Grandpa's disappearance, but at that point I don't know for sure what's happened to him. I just need to be around my friends. I need them to take care of me, to tell me our lives will go on as expected, Italy's calling, it will be splendid. But when I think back on that night, I realize I'm there, waiting for Jen and Tammy and Sash at Klein's at 10:30 on a Thursday night because I'll need their help to learn the language I'll be forced to use in the days to come, the tongue of the missing.

Fifteen minutes pass and my friends haven't arrived. When the waiter brings the cigarettes, I no longer feel like smoking. My brain feels twice its original size. I'm sitting at the table we always use during our conversations with Diane, overlooking the constant traffic jam on Masaryk. At the crêperie across the street, a couple's been making out on the terrace since I arrived. I can't see her face because her back is to me, but I could swear it's Diane. I discard the idea. I can see his face and I simply can't believe that he could be the man for whom she traded a life of glamour and sophistication in Milan. He's slightly older than me and not especially handsome or refined. He's wearing a hideous brown suit that fits him terribly, like cheap clothing always does. He could be a bank teller or an insurance sales-man, so she definitely can't be Diane—also, she could be his mother, for Christ's sake! I always imagined the Italian polyglot dating a seasoned hedge fund manager, the irresistible cultural attaché of some exotic country or a renowned salt-and-pepper chef, but I'd never once considered she could fall for *that*. He beckons the waiter, waving the check-please sign in the air, while she fixes up her hair and takes a little mirror out of her purse and corrects her rouge. It's her. In my mind, Grandpa's now saying, "Please don't hurt me, I'll give you whatever you want. Please!" and I feel tears rolling down my cheeks. The waiter arrives with the check and the bank teller or the insur-ance salesman pays with cash. Next they rise and head down the street, and I can now see her face, radiant and full of peace. Diane rests her head on the ill-fitting shoulder pad of his suit and holds his hand as they walk away. She's never looked more beautiful and triumphant. Grandpa's lips are now bleeding, one of the fat guys has just punched him in the face. My hands are trembling, my heart's about to blow. I still refuse to believe that the bank teller or the insurance salesman loves Diane back the same, but they stop and kiss under the pale moonlight of the night the city turned its back on me, and it astounds me to see how little they need to feel like a million bucks.

# OKIE

Ms. Brinkman said that writing could help, and handed me a notebook. She was sitting on her desk, and I was standing in front of it. The other kids were already on the playground. She called it a journal, and said she had one at home. She wrote in it every night. Some nights, she said, it's just a paragraph about a special moment I enjoyed during the day, others, I can write pages on end. It makes those happy moments even more memorable, she said, and it makes those not so happy ones feel less important. After I read them on the page I realize they're not such a big deal, she said, and smiled. The classroom smelled like new carpet and sharpened pencils. Third grade had just started, and I was the only new kid in class. Ms. Brinkman said I didn't have to show her what I wrote. Just write, sweetie. If you feel like showing it to me, I'll be happy to read it. If you don't, that's okay. If you feel like talking about it, that would be great as well.

I came home that night and told Josefina what Ms. Brinkman had said. I showed her the notebook. I explained that Ms. Brinkman had called it a journal. What's the difference, Josefina asked. I'm not sure, I said. I guess you write regular stuff in a notebook and important stuff in a journal? Josefina wanted to know if I was going to use it. I don't know, I said. It's beautiful, she said. We were packed into the kitchen of the tiny house we'd just moved into. Josefina was loading the dishwasher with frying pans. She'd just learned how to use it. Why do you think she gave it to you? Just because, I guess? I replied. Josefina said what she always did. Don't lie to me, Bernardo. I know you. You can fool everybody but me. Please don't tell my parents, I said. Why would I? she asked. I don't know. Have I ever told them something you've asked me not to? No. Why would I start now? I don't know, I said. We're here now. So? Things are different now. I'm not different. I'm the same old Josefina. I supposed that was true. She kept wearing the blue-and-white uniform she did back home, she still braided her long black hair, she still looked sweaty all the time. Are you going to tell me why she gave it to you? I don't participate much in class. I don't speak with anybody at school. Why's that? That's what Ms. Brinkman wanted to know. So, did you tell her? No. I just don't feel like talking to anyone here.

After dinner I went to my room and opened the notebook. I had never seen one of these before. It was black-and-white and sturdy, and had the word Composition printed on the cover. I stared at the white page. Mom's taking swimming lessons in the same pool as me, I wrote. I don't like it. I closed the notebook and put it in my backpack. When my parents and my little brother were asleep I went to Josefina's room. She was still awake, already in her flannel gown decorated with daisies, reading the Bible. Her room smelled like the rose hand cream she always applied after doing dishes. Hers was not in the back, away from ours, like at home, but next to the kitchen, and looked like any other room in the house. All the rooms, including hers, had rough beige carpet on the floor. If you knocked on the walls, even on the tiled ones in the bathroom, they sounded hollow and flimsy, as if they were made out of cardboard. I slipped into Josefina's bed. It was cozy with the warmth of her big body. You've got to stop doing this, she said. If your parents find out they are going to be mad at me. I snuggled next to her. She sighed. She stroked my hair. Her hands looked older than the rest of her body. She put her palms together and I did too. We prayed Our Father and she turned off the lights.

She woke me up early the next morning, before my parents had opened the door to their room. I went back to my bed and pretended to sleep while Josefina fixed breakfast for me and my brother.

A few days later, Ms. Brinkman asked me to stay in the classroom at the start of recess. When we were alone she asked me how the writing was coming along. It's going okay, I said. Is it helping? I don't know. Well, keep at it, sweetie. Have you made any new friends? I didn't reply. Every time she called me sweetie I felt like a Muppet. That's just fine, Ms. Brinkman said. It takes time, you know? My family lived in Oklahoma until I was six, and then we moved to California. It wasn't easy, she said. You know what kids called me at school? They called me Okie. And it was almost the eighties. It took time. And now, look at me: I'm a true California girl, she said, but I didn't note anything particular about the way she looked. I'd never heard that word before, Okie. I didn't know what it meant. Ms. Brinkman had brown, curly hair, her eyes were so blue they looked like a doll's. She dressed in those long colorful handmade dresses tourists like to buy from street vendors in Vallarta or Cabo. She smiled all the time. You'll get the hang of it, sweetie, she insisted.

I was alone, sitting on a bench away from the basketball courts, where the other kids played during recess, when a girl from class came over. Her hair was beyond blond, it was almost white. She was tall and very skinny. You're weird, she said. Excuse me? I said you're weird. I didn't reply. See? You're weird. If you weren't weird you'd say something back.

I only noticed Mom didn't know how to swim when we moved to California. One day, while she was driving to the pool, I asked her why she had to take swimming lessons now. Because I want to learn, she said. But why? Because before I was afraid of the water, and I don't want to be anymore. But why do you have to take lessons in the same pool, next to me? I like it, that we get to do something together. What's wrong with that? she asked. It's weird. Mom laughed. Weird? Where did you get that?

It was after ten that night when Josefina put her Bible down and her palms together, and so did I. Why are we here? I asked when the lights were out. Why do you have to ask the same thing every night, Bernardo? Because I want to know. I told you already. Your mom and your dad decided to move, and asked me to come with you. They didn't explain why. It's none of my business. That's not true, I said. You know why we moved but you don't want to tell me. Josefina had cooked entomatadas for dinner that evening, and something about her, her hands or her clothes, smelled like poached onion, which made me think of home. Have I ever lied to you? I don't know. Watch your mouth, young man, or else I'll kick you out of my room. Have I ever lied to you?

The same girl approached me at recess again. What's up, weirdo? Are you weird because you're Mexican, or are you

weird just because you're a weirdo? I was sitting on the bench. She stood in front of me, casting a shadow on my head. Are you ugly because you're güera or just because you're ugly? I said back to her. What did you call me? I didn't reply. Repeat what you just said or else I'm telling Ms. Brinkman. If you tell her that I'll tell her you're calling me weirdo. What did you call me? Güera. What does that mean? If you don't know, that's your problem, güereja. It was awesome, the face she made.

Days later, one of the kids in my swimming class asked me why my mom was taking lessons there too, if grown-ups where I came from didn't know how to swim. On the way home I told her that I wanted her to stop. Why would you ask me to do that? The kids in my group are teasing me. Why? Because you don't know how to swim. Well, she said. She looked at herself in the rearview mirror and fixed her hair. It was still damp and messy from the pool and looked darker than usual. Next time they tease you, tell them to do it in Spanish. When they learn to tease you in Spanish, I'll stop taking swimming lessons there.

A few nights later I wrote in the notebook: Her name's Ambrose and she showed up again today. She came over and looked at me but she didn't say anything at first. What? I said. Nothing, I'm just looking at you, she said. Well, I'm not a monkey in a zoo, so stop looking at me, I said. She chuckled. You are. You're a weird monkey. You're a baboon. It was funny, the way she said it. Stop calling me weird. I don't like it.

The next day, Josefina came to pick me up. Instead of her uniform, she wore her Sunday best, as if she were going to church. It made me happy to see her at school, but I wanted to know where Mom was. She said she was at the ER with my brother. His kindergarten teacher had called to report that Maximiliano had jumped off the top of the slide and his arm didn't look good. Back home, Josefina never would have picked me up just because Mom couldn't. One of my aunts, or Dad's chauffeur, would have. When Mom and Max came home that afternoon, his left arm was in a cast. He showed me the lollipops the nurses gave him for being such a sport. They were bright purple and green. That night I wrote in the notebook: Max is nuts. I'm sure he did that thing on the slide on purpose. I'm sure he doesn't like it here either.

A few nights later Josefina asked if I was writing a lot in my notebook. Not much, just a couple things. Can you tell me what you've been writing about? Silly stuff, that's all. C'mon, tell me. If I do, do you promise not to tell anyone? It's old Josefina you're talking to, Bernardo, what kind of question is that? I told her I was writing about taking swimming lessons with Mom, and how much I hated it. Well, if I were you, I'd be proud of her, she said. You need to be very brave to do that when you're a grown-up. Why? I asked. Because fear's like a spell, Bernardo, fear can be paralyzing. I know what it's like. I don't know how to swim either. I imagined Josefina taking swimming lessons in the same pool, with me and Mom. I wish I were brave enough to do what she's doing. You should be proud of her, she repeated. You should be proud of your parents, Bernardo. They are very brave people.


A few days later I wrote in the notebook: I lied. Ambrose is not ugly, she's actually very pretty. Today I told her that and apologized for being mean to her. I mean, I didn't say she was pretty. I just said I didn't mean to call her ugly. She said I'd called her some other name too. I said I'd called her blondie. What's wrong with that? she said. Nothing, I said. Well, I still think you're weird, she said, but like, good weird, you know?

What's the difference? I asked. I don't know, she said. There's just a difference.

I see you're now friends with Ambrose, Ms. Brinkman said during our weekly talk. This time we sat in the corner where we usually had story time, surrounded by shiny red, green, yellow, and purple square pillows. I told you it was just a matter of time, sweetie. I nodded. How's the writing coming along? It's going okay. Is it helping you feel better here, more at home? It was so annoying, the way she'd ask me questions. This is not home, I said. I'm feeling better, but this is not home. Ms. Brinkman made like she was going to touch my hair, but she didn't. It will be, sweetie, she said. Even though it's hard for you to see it now, it will.

After my talk with Ms. Brinkman I went to the playground and found Ambrose sitting on the bench where we always met, like she was waiting for me. I told her about Mom taking swimming lessons. She swims from one side of the pool to the other holding a Styrofoam board with lots of colors on it, kicking the water hard. It's just ridiculous, I said. Why do you hate it so much? My mom's taking yoga classes where she's with a bunch of people in a room that's like, five hundred degrees, and everybody's sweating like roasted chickens. Now, that's embarrassing. And gross, I said. Exactly. What's wrong with taking swimming lessons? Nothing. I just don't like that she's there at the same time I am. Does she wear floaties or something? We giggled. No, she doesn't, but still.

That night I asked Josefina if she missed Mexico. She said she sometimes did, but not every day. She said she liked Palo Alto, she liked that she could walk to the grocery store without worrying that someone would snatch her purse or mug her. She liked that she could take the bus to church and no one messed with her, that the house where we now lived had a dishwasher so she didn't have to scrub all the dishes by hand, but she did miss her sisters and visiting her hometown on weekends. I asked her if she wanted to go back. She thought about it, looking at her Bible. She'd already stuck pictures of her family and a laminated poster of the Sacred Heart of Jesus to the wall above her bed. Hers was the only decorated room in the house. I've always lived with your family. I've known you and Maxie since the day you were born, you were the size of a butternut squash the first time I held you in my hands, and just as heavy. We giggled. You're like my children, she said. Josefina didn't have kids or a husband, not even a boyfriend. If she ever did, I never met them. Do you think we'll ever go back? I asked. I don't know, Bernardo. Yes, you do. You just don't want to tell me. You calling me a liar, young man?

I've been thinking about your mom and her swimming lessons, Ambrose said at recess a few days later. She said she knew how to make her stop. You need to embarrass her in front of everybody at the pool. I asked her if she did that with her own mom. Sure, it works all the time. But you have to really embarrass her, like, really bad, like, OMG. I wasn't sure if she was right. I wasn't sure if I wanted to do that. Even if I did, how would I do it? Well, you need to come up with a plan, baboon, Ambrose said. Plan it out, man. I liked the way she called me baboon, but I didn't tell her.

The weather began to get colder. I started to participate in class, replying to simple questions Ms. Brinkman asked. She was happy. She said we no longer needed to meet every week. I was so excited to be off the hook I wanted to hug her. But if you feel like talking, you can always come see me, sweetie. My door's always open. I nodded. How's the writing coming along?

I stopped writing, I said. Ms. Brinkman looked serious at first, but then she smiled, as always. Well, that's probably because you don't need it anymore, right? I nodded. You can go back to it if you feel like, sweetie. Writing's always a great help.

Dad had dinner with us that evening. Most evenings he didn't. His job at the university kept him busy. Josefina was serving flan for dessert when I asked my parents if we were going back to Mexico City for the holidays. Dad didn't answer, instead he said he was thinking we could spend the winter break in Hawaii. He said some colleagues at Stanford told him it was a fantastic place for Christmas. Mom said it was a great idea. I've heard the weather's gorgeous there that time of the year, she said. But we always spend Christmas at Grandpa's, I said. Yeah, Grandpa!, said Max completely out of the blue. Mom and Dad looked at each other. He said they were doing renovations at Grandpa's this year so we'd have to wait. We can celebrate at our house or with our uncles and aunts, I insisted. Josefina came out of the kitchen and asked who wanted a second helping of flan. She never offered second helpings of dessert when my parents had dinner with us, but that evening she did.

I spent that night and the next lying on my bed, figuring out my plan. Both nights I lost track of time, and when I went to Josefina's room she was asleep. I slipped into her bed and pushed her big body with mine so I could fit in. She moved over but didn't wake up. The morning after the second night, Josefina didn't ask what I wanted for breakfast, she just grabbed the first box of cereal she found in the pantry and served me a bowl with cold milk. There's something going on and you're not telling me, Bernardo, she said. I know you. You can't fool Josefina. I didn't reply. I wanted to tell her what was keeping me busy at night, but I couldn't.

Ambrose offered to help with the plan, but I said it was

23

okay. I felt embarrassed to share the details with her. I was afraid it wouldn't be good enough. She asked if I was ready for the big day. I said I thought I was. Well, good luck, baboon, she said. It made me uneasy, the way she said it.

It happened on a Monday. Before heading to my swimming lesson, I went to the bathroom, removed the one-liter bottle of sparkling water I had kept hidden in the cabinet, and drank it all in one big gulp. Mom had to wait for me in the car. When I finally jumped in, I couldn't help a burp. She asked if everything was okay. I said it was. We didn't say anything else on our way to the pool.

We were halfway through the lesson when my bladder started to hurt. Mom was a couple lanes away, doing free-style kick laps, holding her colorful board. Her coach complimented her technique. Good job, Carolina! the coach shouted. At the end of the lesson, my own coach was giving our group feedback on butterfly and backstroke, the styles we'd practiced that day, when I crept out of the pool and stood by the edge. Coach gave me a half smile. I waited for Mom to reach the far side of the pool, and when she did, I called her name. Mom! Mom! I yelled. She took off her goggles, gave me a big grin, and waved. Everyone was looking at me. I pulled my swimsuit down, and aimed for coach. The shot of pee reached target on her swim cap, right at the beginning of her hairline, and splashed on her collarbone, her chest, the tip of her nose. She shrieked and sprang back away from me. It looked like she was moving in slow motion through the water. I aimed for the kids. They began to wiggle and twitch and scream. Coach called my name. One of the kids started crying for his mom. Bernardo! coach yelled. Bernardo! I looked at her. Stop! she yelled. Stop! I couldn't, even if I'd wanted to. I had to look away. More screams erupted. If Mom started screaming too I didn't know, I couldn't see her reaction, my eyes were now shut. My face was burning.

I stayed by the edge of the pool with my eyes closed. My swimsuit pooled around my ankles, cold and itchy. It felt like a long time passed before I heard Mom approaching me, yelling I'm sorry! I'm sorry! so loud it sounded as if she were apologizing to every person in the pool. She pulled up my swimsuit, wrapped me in a towel, and whisked me out the door. She didn't say anything to me. She just kept yelling I'm sorry! I'm sorry! imploringly.

When we reached the car, I was shivering. I didn't remember the last time Mom had spanked me. I opened my eyes, expecting to see rage on her face, but I found her wrapped in a towel herself, damp and disheveled, covering her wet face. She managed to pull herself together and asked me to change my clothes inside the car. Then she asked me to wait on the sidewalk while she changed. It was cold outside, and getting dark. Okay, how about a burger and a milkshake? she proposed once we were both in the car. She sounded exhausted. I didn't reply. I didn't know what to say. I wondered if I'd ever be able to look her in the eye again. She took out her cell phone, called home, and told Josefina that she and I were dining out. She asked her to serve Max dinner and make sure he was in bed by eight thirty.


Mom drove downtown. On our way back from swimming lessons she'd usually turn on the radio and listen to the news, but that evening she played classical music. She parked on the street and we walked in silence to the Palo Alto Creamery. Mom asked for a booth. She sat on one side and I on the other, facing each other. When the waitress brought us the menus Mom said I could order whatever I wanted. I ordered a chili burger and an Oreo cookie extra-thick milkshake with whipped cream and hot fudge. Excellent choice! the waitress said as she wrote on her little pad. Mom ordered chicken noodle soup and asked to see the wine list. The waitress said they didn't have one. Mom ordered tea.

Okay, Bernardo, what's going on? Mom asked after the waitress left. I didn't reply at first. She said she wasn't mad, but she would be if I didn't tell her the truth. I cleared my throat. I want you to stop taking swimming lessons with me. My voice came out low and shaky. She sighed. You know that's bullshit, don't you? She'd never used that word with me before. I want the truth, Bernardo. Please. She said it like she was begging. Her face looked like she hadn't slept in weeks. I don't like it here. My face blushed. Our house is too small. I miss our home. I miss my cousins, and my friends, and Grandpa. I miss them too, Mom said. She sounded like she'd aged decades in the last two hours. I don't know what we're doing here, and every time I ask why we moved or when we're going back home everybody ignores me or lies to me. I hate it, I said, and started to cry. I couldn't fight back the tears, and I was embarrassed. Mom looked like she was about to start weeping too and inched around the table and embraced me. She whispered my name a couple times as she buried my head in her chest. It was warm. To my surprise, it didn't smell like chlorine. It smelled like perfume, like flowers. We stayed like that until the waitress showed up again.

Alrighty! The waitress placed our food in front of us and shuffled things around on the table so that Mom didn't have to withdraw. Enjoy, folks! the waitress said, and left. Mom took a spoonful of soup and said it was good. She asked if I wanted to try it. I said no thanks. I took a bite of the burger. It tasted chewy and sweet. I didn't finish it.

I know how you feel, Bernardo, Mom said after we had finished eating. Telling lies is not okay, but explaining why we're here is not easy. All you and your brother need to know is that Dad and I love you guys very much. We're doing this for you. Tell me why we're here, Mom. Please. She looked like she was going to say something, but stopped. I insisted. Please, please, please, please. Okay! she said, raising her voice. But you cannot repeat any of this to Maxie, and you cannot tell your father we talked about this. He'd kill me if he ever finds out. I nodded. Her face changed. She thought for a while. Then she said there were some mean people in Mexico who wanted to take everything we had away from us. They started calling home every day to say that if we didn't give them what they wanted they'd harm us or you guys, or even Grandpa. We couldn't let that happen, she said. So, we had to get some distance. We'll have to spend some time here, until those people forget about us. I wanted to know why those people would want to take what was ours and why we couldn't do anything to make them stop. I wanted to know how long we'd have to wait before we could go back, but Mom didn't give me time to ask. She looked at her watch and said it was late. She asked for the check. Things will be fine, Bernardo, I promise, she said. Things will get better. It will be fun to discover this new place. Don't you like it here, even a little bit? Isn't it gorgeous? I just nodded. As we headed to the car we stood outside the restaurant and she gave me a hug like she hadn't in a while. My baby, my poor baby, she whispered in my ear.

. . .

On our way back home Mom wanted to know what had happened at the pool. I said I was sorry. I wanted to say something else, but I didn't. I couldn't. First Mom said that of course it could never ever happen again. She tried to sound severe. That was a strange and stupid thing to do, Bernardo, she then said with her regular voice, looking at me through the rearview mirror. Where did you get that idea? I didn't reply. It was so embarrassing, Bernardo. What were you thinking? We'll have to send that poor coach some flowers. You'll have to write her a note, okay? And those poor kids! And their parents! Oh, my God, Bernardo! She sounded concerned, but I couldn't help feeling that she was about to laugh. We can't go back to that pool, I said. That's for sure, she said. But we'll find another one, Bernardo. It's not the end of the world.

Mom, I said when she parked the car outside the house, does Josefina know why we're here? She looked at me through the rearview mirror with the car keys in her hand. She said Josefina had been with us forever. She said it was as if she were part of the family. God only knows the things Josefina knows about us, Bernardo.

That night the light in Josefina's room remained on till late. I knew she was waiting for me. I wanted to go in there, snuggle next to her, and tell her everything about that day, what had happened at the pool, how much I feared going to school the next day. I wanted to tell her what Mom had said at the Creamery, what she'd said in the car, and how I felt. But I didn't. I closed the door to my room, got in my bed, and turned out the lights. But I couldn't sleep. I had to turn them back on.

# ORIGAMI PRUNES

I first met Laura at a washateria the day both my washer and Michael Jackson died. It was the end of June, Austin gusty and yellowed in heat, orange in the sky. Wildfires were consuming the Hill Country, and local TV anchors had started to talk about the end of the world. It was Thursday and for no reason, I had called in sick.

"First time in a laundromat?" I chose that word because it sounded nicer than washateria, and because the moment I spotted Laura I felt the urge to impress her. I knew immediately where she came from. People like us recognize each other from miles away, we overdressed outcasts adrift in middle-of-nowhere America.

"Why, yes," she said in Spanish, glaring dismissively at the buttons on the washer's control panel.

"These guys are a piece of cake, unlike the one I'm sure you have at home."

"Like I know how *that* one works."

"Of course." I smiled.

"May I ask why are you doing this yourself?" I said. "Why didn't you ask one of your domestics?" I wondered if she employed in-house servants in Austin as she surely had back in Mexico, or if she could now only afford them by the hour. I wondered if hers was one of those families that brought their longtime maids with them from home and then, once abroad, called them *au pairs*. I wondered how many servants she had on payroll before, how many remained, and if she cried at night for her loss.

"Ugh," she hissed as she threw clean, perfectly folded clothes into the machine. "Don't get me started."

Laura's helplessness was wrapped in a thin layer of arrogance that made her sexy and unnerving, a thing you wanted to put your hands on. She'd dyed her hair the color of an explosion in the sun. I thought it made her look older than she was. She wore single white pearl earrings. You can tell a woman's true class by the way she wears pearls, Grandma would say. Diamonds are flashy and expensive, an easy bet. Pearls are different. Pearls are hard to pull off.

She'd forgotten to bring detergent and softener, and so had I. I bought two single-load packets of Tide and a small bottle of Downy at the vending machine, and got both washers going. The laundromat was cool and almost empty. Besides us, there was an elderly Asian man folding one synthetic-fabric sports shirt after another, and an obese young Latina with two little girls who played tag all over the place, filling the room with giggles and yells. They were loud and annoying, but we didn't have the nerve to give the mom a look. "These people are hopeless," was all Laura said.

We sat facing a long line of mammoth dryers with glass doors, and waited. Two large flat-screen TVs showed a muted news segment on Detroit's auto industry, the same soundless images repeating themselves on a loop, like a recurring dream. I glimpsed at the screens from time to time, but Laura ignored them. We watched jeans and panties and skirts roll in soothing twirls of hot air as they dried in the big machines, a troupe of dancers flying and tumbling together, as if their owners' bodies had broken free, vanishing into merrier realms.

"Where are you from?" I asked.

"Mexico City."

"I know that."

Laura grinned.

"I mean, which part of the city?"

"Which part do you think I'm from?"

Crow's-feet branched from the corner of her eyes. She wore very little makeup—unusual for a Mexican housewife. Michael Jackson was minutes from the end and the larger world was about to change. Ours too, but I didn't know it. She did. Laura's plump body was clad in a navy linen dress decorated with water lilies that played nicely with the vintage mustard Gucci bag that lay on top of the washer, like an aardvark in a cattle ranch. Every time I remember Laura in that dress, my balls tingle.

"You look south."

She let out a small laugh.

"You're doing well, country boy. Keep going."

"San Angel, I'd say."

She giggled and looked out the window. Had she just called me country boy?

"I grew up in Polanco, but moved to Chimalistac when I married. His family always lived there." Laura stood and reached for her purse. She retrieved her phone and ran a finger up and down the screen, pretending to check her messages. I took out my phone and started to imitate her every move. I wondered about the color of her nipples.

Like Laura, I still lived under the weight of having fled the city where I was born. I worked for the Department of Protection for Mexican Nationals of the Consulate, running dead-end errands like visiting undocumented immigrants awaiting deportation, pretending to make them feel cared for. The Secretaría de Relaciones Exteriores had just transferred me from Raleigh to Austin. I had moved to Raleigh from Mexico City because my parents had begged me to take the job in the Mexican Foreign Service that Dad had secured for me. They'd recently moved to La Jolla themselves, tired of seeing friend after friend disappear in broad daylight, exhausted from wondering each morning when their number would be called. I didn't want to leave. I was cutting my teeth as a reporter for *El Financiero*, but Dad said that letting me stay was the same as their not leaving Mexico at all.

In the days after I moved to North Carolina, I started having dreams that my friends from Mexico would ring me from Butner asking for help, but when I called the prison I'd learn that they'd already been deported to an undisclosed location. I started dreaming of Grandma, clad in one of the bright silky dresses she liked so much that smelled of baby powder. I'd see her in her living room, knitting, singing "Solamente Una Vez" as if the bolero were a lullaby. She died alone in her apartment on Cofre de Perote on a winter morning the year after I moved.

"Let me see your hands," Laura said. I offered them to her, palms up.

She held them carefully at first, as if getting acquainted with an alien object. She massaged my knuckles with her longest fingers and my palms with her thumbs, maternally; fingertips tepid and unused, the color of raw pork meat.

"Beautiful hands," she said. "So soft and young. How old are you?"

"Twenty-six."

She looked me in the eye, and chuckled.

"I'm forty-five," she said. "There. I said it. Now let's pretend I didn't."

"I'm cool with that," I said, my hands still in hers.

"Anything else you may want to know before we move on?"

"You said you're married."

"I am." She sighed, her face sagged. "We moved to Austin five years ago, but he still spends most of his time in Mexico. Taking care of the business, or so he says. We have two girls, one finishing college, the other starting. They're both on the East Coast. I'm stuck here, in this big, supercosmopolitan metropolis full of pickup trucks, where you may run into vultures and deer on every corner. Lovely, isn't it?"

I wanted to ask why she'd left Mexico, but I didn't.

"So, which part of the city are *you* from?" Laura's face got playful again.

"Are you gonna guess my neighborhood by abusing my hands?"

"Why not?" She smelled like classic perfume, perhaps Chanel No. 5. "Are you afraid of a human's touch? Have you become that American already?"

"It's not that, ma'am. I just wanna show a little resistance. I think you'll like that."

"You're definitely south. Jardines del Pedregal?"

I laughed. I put my hands in my pockets and swiftly kissed her on the cheek. Her skin was a peach.

Later, we saw our own clean clothes tumble away inside the machines. She rested her head on my shoulder.

"Give me your phone," she said.

Laura pointed the camera toward us, her slender naked arm outstretched, her flesh loose and freckled, and brought her face close to mine. She closed her eyes, and took the first snapshot. In the days that followed we'd photograph each other like crazy. Pictures of us eating raw octopus; pictures of us in bed taken against the burning background of the hills. Pictures of me caressing the side of her breasts. What would her daughters say if they saw these photos? I'd ask. What about her husband? She'd say she didn't care, and keep snapping, amour fou–style.

She pretended to lick at my ear and said:

"One more. Say por vida!"

The laundromat was filling up with young hipster couples, middle-aged men, and frumpy single mothers, children hot on their trail. There was something tragic about washing your clothes in front of others, and I wondered why Laura would be here voluntarily.

"You haven't told me your name yet."

"Plutarco. Plutarco Mills."

"A portentous name for a dashing young man," Laura said. "I think we don't speak the same lingua anymore, Mr. Mills." From then on, she always called me by my last name. It turned me on. The sound of my name on her lips made my limbs and ears rattle. Had I known what would happen afterward, I'd have recorded her voice with my phone.

"Yes we do," I contested. "Not only do we speak the same language, we also respond to the same impulse." Listening to Laura made me feel at home: she twisted statements into questions that turned doubt into a familiar space.

"No, we don't, Mr. Mills. You're young and still believe in things like love and the future. I don't have the stomach to prove you wrong, not as long as my wrists are attached to my hands, but this you must know," she said, and paused. "The main difference between us and other couples is not what you think, those naughty clichés working up your cute little brain that make me yawn. The main difference between us, Mr. Mills, and them, all of them, is that the words that come out of your mouth, even the simplest ones, ripen into origami prunes in my heart."

I imagined my tongue inside her mouth, swollen purple and moist. The dryers buzzed, and our hot clothes collapsed to the bottom of the machines as if life had suddenly been sucked out of them.

"Would you like to go out with me, Mr. Mills?" she asked as we pulled them out and tossed them back into plastic baskets, two jumbles of color and undistinguishable fabric that made no sense.

We walked out into the hazy afternoon air. It felt heavy and metallic in the mouth. The unexpected taste of smog and burnt debris that arrived in gusts brought me back to Mexico City. Laura looked up and took a deep breath, and I realized we both felt the same. Nostalgia is the saddest form of glee.

"One more thing," she said by the door of her black Porsche Cayenne. "Condoms? Don't bother. I couldn't care less."

"What if *I* care?"

"Let me ask you something, Mr. Mills," Laura said, the commanding words not matching the sudden frail tone of her voice. "This game won't have many rounds. Are you man enough to let the lady take the lead?"


"Mr. Mills!" Laura yelled on the phone. "We've got to celebrate!"

It was noon on Friday and we weren't supposed to meet until Saturday. The news that day was full of rumors that Michael Jackson had taken his own life and reports that the

Hill Country wildfires were reaching the shores of Lake Travis. Firemen from every corner of Texas and Oklahoma rushed in our direction as Jackson's classics from the seventies and eighties topped the charts.

"And why is that?"

"Surprise, surprise! Can we meet now?"

"I'm in the middle of something," I said quietly so that only she could hear me.

I was at the Brackenridge Hospital, translating for a family from Estado de México whose teenage son had been badly beaten the night before outside a gay bar on East César Chávez, and later dropped off by anonymous friends outside the emergency room. The kid's mother was chubby and small. She looked devastated, her skin the color of cardboard blistered by the Texas heat. Her husband wore a ragged Longhorns cap, and explained that they were from Ixtlahuaca. I'd probably never heard of it, he said, but I had because most of the maids from home came from there. He'd been living in Austin for several years, but his son and wife had arrived only the year before. The boy was seventeen but had always shown a great talent for the arts, he said. The word *arts* sounded foreign in his mouth. He wanted to be a filmmaker; in recent months he'd been working on his first project, championed by his art teacher at school. "Teachers *adore* him," the father said. The movie was titled *Zombies and Narcos vs. Aliens*, and was about zombies who are about to take over a small Mexican town controlled by a ferocious drug cartel when an extraterrestrial attack strikes. "He didn't know who prevailed in the end," the father said, his wobbly cheeks glossy wet and flushed. He looked insignificant and fragile in spite of his sunburnt, strong, hairless arms. I sucked at my job. I didn't know how to comfort these people, how to make them believe that things would get better, because most of the time, they didn't. I translated the doctor's prognosis, that the kid had received too many kicks to the head, that the skull presented several fissures, and that the boy had slipped into an irreversible coma. My phone rang, and I asked them to excuse me for a minute. When I heard Laura's voice, I felt grateful and safe, and cowardly.

"Can we meet tonight then?" she asked.

"Sure," I said. "Where?"

She said the laundromat. "I'll bring some clothes, and we'll celebrate while we watch them dry. How about that?"

Years later, I still consider her words. I now divine longing and anxiety in her voice, but in that moment all I found was Laura's unleashed self, a storm impossible to contain, an energy that made me want to laugh and be with her, to see her bare.

When I returned to the hospital room the parents were now sitting on plastic chairs, looking hopelessly down at the floor.


Laura walked into the washateria around seven carrying a basketful of clothes masterfully folded. She wore a narrow white dress and copper sandals with wedge heels. When she saw me, she dropped the basket on the floor, grabbed me by the hand, and dragged me outside.

She opened the trunk of her SUV to reveal a small cooler filled with ice, two fuchsia thermoses, and a bottle of Taittinger Brut Millésimé 1998.

"I didn't want to overdo it, so real flutes were out of the question," she said like the gracious host of a cocktail party apologizing for the mind-blowing hors d'oeuvres. "People'll think we're drinking iced tea." She handed me the bottle of champagne.

"You're so definitely north."

"Shut up." Laura cracked up as I poured bubbles. "Okay, let's make a toast!"

"To what?"

"To this gorgeous Jean Paul Gaultier, that I got at Neiman today," she said, gently pulling down the neck of her dress to show me a sliver of cream-colored ruffles, and clinked her thermos on mine. The evening air was nuclear hot, we were alone in the parking lot, and nothing moved, nothing else made a sound. I felt like we were the only ones left in Austin, the only ones left in the world.

"Are you serious?" I said, and let out a nervous laugh.

"Oh, absolutely, Mr. Mills. But wait, there's more."

"I'm all ears, ma'am."

"I'll let those beautiful hands of yours unhook it for me tonight," she whispered in my ear.

Before I could reply she kissed me on the lips for the first time, the childish kiss of a trembling gal is how I remember it now, but in that moment all I felt was her wetness on mine and a quick hard-on. She refilled our thermoses and dragged me back inside the Laundromat.

We separated our clothes into two categories, white and everything else, and dumped each pile into a dryer. We cranked the machines and took a seat to watch each load create a distinctive palette while tumbling, makeshift flutes in one hand and in the other each other's, like a couple of inexperienced schoolkids. My thoughts raced imagining the texture of her underwear.

"White or colored?"

"White's so balmy."

"I know, right? But colored is like, rough and intense, and like, *sexy*."

"It is." She sighed.

"Balmy or sexy? Choose one."

"I can't," Laura said. "I just love seeing all those clothes fly away. I wish I could do the same."

We grew quiet. I felt Laura so close to me, closer than anyone else had ever been; her body washing all over me in waves of heat.

"You can, if you want to," I said, shaking my thermos; it was empty now.

"It's not so easy, Mr. Mills." Her voice soured. "You think it is, because you're juvenile and unharmed, but it's not."

"Actually, it *is*. I can make that happen for you, ma'am. I can stand in front of the dryer while you're inside, so that the manager doesn't notice."

"Are you kidding me?" She stared at me, stunned. For once, I felt older, stronger.

"I've never been more serious, ma'am. I can try it myself first. If something's not right, I'll just swing the door open."

A big mischievous grin spread across her face.

"Would you do that for me, Mr. Mills?" she asked girlishly and ran a long, perfectly French-manicured index finger down my slender biceps.

"You said you'll let me dispose of your undies tonight, ma'am. It's the least I can do."

We took the clothes out of the dryers, and dumped them into a metal basket on wheels. We waited for the manager to retreat to the back, and then I hopped into the dryer. Laura and I agreed that the cool-air cycle would be the safest. Once I was inside, she wheeled the metallic basket in front of the dryer and pretended to make herself busy with our clothes.

"Watch your head, Mr. Mills," she whispered before closing the door. I knew then what Laika felt like when she was launched into orbit—that damned solitary dog and I, two little furry animals searching for unknown forms of life in outer space.

The first couple of spins were rough as my body adjusted to the metallic hardness of this new habitat. The air was itchy and had an artificial, eerie taste to it. It felt leaden in my lungs as if I were breathing from an air tank filled with morning breath. But then the space flattened out and the air cleared, the sense of flying in circles vanished, and I broke free. My body felt light as if made only of cartilage, the direction of my flight determined by subtle movements of my limbs and nose and brows. I hovered over the big city, savoring a bubblegum taste in the air I didn't remember it had. I recognized the rooftop of the house I grew up in and the tennis courts of the country club where I learned to ride on horseback and where I almost drowned at four, and the lush, infinite garden where I saw myself and Grandma on the lawn, holding a book from *Les Aventures de Tintin* in her pouchy hands, my head resting on her lap.

Then the muffled yells of the manager broke into the dryer. When the machine stopped I fell hard to the bottom; one hundred and eighty pounds of flesh and bone back in my body all at once. I was hot and claustrophobic.

"What the fuck are you people doing?" The pale young woman dressed in a sad blue-gray uniform was now standing in front of the dryer, wide-eyed. "Get the fuck out of there! Now! And you, lady"—she turned to Laura, whose face I couldn't see because I was desperately trying to hop out of the dryer—"you should be ashamed of yourself! At your age!"

Customers of all ages and ethnicities and fabric preferences looked on amused as the manager escorted us out the door.

"If I ever see you two here again, I swear to God I'll call the police!" she shouted as she threw Laura's basket of jumbled clothes into the parking lot.

"Are you okay?" Laura asked.

"I am. It's just that some people don't have a sense of humor at all. Tant pis."

"I'm not talking about her, Mr. Mills," she said worriedly. "Are you sure you're not hurt?"

"Yeah, I'm perfectly fine."

"The sounds of your body hitting against that drum were unbearable. That's why the manager noticed, but I freaked out and didn't know how to turn the damn thing off. Even a couple of women started to scream when they saw you tumbling like a bag of potatoes in there," Laura said, containing a laugh.

"Well, ma'am," I said as I combed my hair back in place with my fingers, feeling suddenly full of life. "You gotta give it a try."

"The poor girl said she'd call the cops on us. I don't feel like getting myself a *mug shot* tonight, Mr. Mills," Laura said.

"My dryer at home works fine," I replied. "It's not as big, but I'm sure you'll fit in."


An amber night had settled in the city by the time we arrived at my place. I lived on the fourteenth floor of a brand-new apartment building on Second Street. Laura tumbled flimsily inside my dryer for almost five minutes, until I worried that the lack of air or the adrenaline rush would keep her from feeling pain, and that the next day she would die from unnoticed bruises or internal bleeding. She stepped out of the machine with a melancholic grin on her face, and we went straight to my room.

She was surprised that I had such a furry butt, and asked me to tell the story about the scar running down my groin. Her dress and the new bra that I'd helped her remove were draped over a chair.

We ordered sushi, and I brought it to bed along with an iced bottle of verdejo. We ate tuna-and-masago maki while she snapped pictures of us nude.

"Why are you here, ma'am?" I finally asked.

"What do you mean?"

"Why did you leave?"

"We were having such a wonderful time, Mr. Mills," she said, motherly. She stroked my leg, then my chest, drawing circles around my nipple with her index finger. "Why ruin it?"

I tried to apologize, but she cut me off.

"I'm teasing you, Mr. Mills. We're all like that. Eventually, we all wonder." She took a sip of wine. A siren howled in the distance. I didn't say a word.

"My father," she said. "He left his office one evening; it was late May. He was supposed to drive home, but he didn't. At first I didn't think there was anything wrong. I thought it was even normal. He was not a kid anymore, his children were all grown-ups now; he was a widow. Why should he come home every single day? What for, to whom? But the next day his assistant called to ask if we knew his whereabouts. He hadn't shown up for work. We called his cell phone, but he wouldn't pick up. We never saw him again. We all had to leave. We didn't know what could happen with us, who could be next."

I thought about saying many things, but none of them felt right. I whispered that I was very sorry.

"I saw him tonight in the dryer, though," Laura went on as if she hadn't heard me. "The moment I was in the air, I headed to Paris—I couldn't help myself," she said. "It was his favorite city. I hovered over Le Marais, looking for him. I spotted him outside L'As, ordering falafel, which was odd because he used to say gar-

42

banzos were food for the poor. I called his name, and he looked up at me; I was floating above him like a lightheaded dragonfly. He seemed embarrassed that I'd found him, but I smiled to show him that he shouldn't be. I've had similar encounters with him in the past, in dreams, always abroad, but nothing like this one. Many times I've dreamt that we bump into each other at the entrance of a department store, Barneys, Selfridges—he's coming out as I'm walking in. His face flushes when he sees me, and he stammers, struggling to explain himself. My joy is so boundless. I kiss him on both cheeks and on the forehead and on the cheeks again, cupping his face in my hands as tightly as if I'd never let him go. The way he looks at me, with those eyes so repentant and sorrowful and yet so free and so alive, makes me believe that he wasn't kidnapped at all, that he ran away."

"Did you get to say something to him this time?"

"I mouthed that he looked dashing, and he seemed moved, but he didn't reply."

Laura's eyes were closed in the scarce light, the expression of her face hard to read. The room smelled like soy sauce and ammonia; her skin, like Downy.

"I wouldn't have the nerve to do that," I said after a while.

"What do you mean?" she asked.

"Leave the people I love behind without notice. Run away from them."

"I'm not saying he did," Laura said with a hint of exasperation in her voice. "But if he'd done that, I wouldn't blame him."

"Why would you want to escape from those you love the most? I don't know if I could forgive someone who did that to me."

"You're such a puppy, Mr. Mills," Laura said, and reached for the sushi. She ate it slowly with her mouth open, making unpleasant noises, as though she'd suddenly become a brat.

"Why would you like to hurt someone so close to you like that?"

"C'mon, Mr. Mills. That's irrelevant—you know that. We're raised to fulfill our big fat last name's expectations, not to make sense of ourselves. But time is unforgiving. And when your belly sags and your skin turns orange, everything else is left to rot. When you grow older and you start realizing that this is it, you don't want to hear things like *I love you* and *Family is everything*. It's okay, but not enough to keep you alive. You want to hear *I want to fuck you*, you want to hear *Life would be meaningless without you*, but you stop hearing that. You wonder whether someone will still find you attractive, whether there's something more exciting than what you settled for, and you want to find it, you want *to make sense of yourself*, but now you have kids, people whose so-called happiness depends on you, the same people you're now teaching to believe in things like love and loyalty and family." The sexy voice was gone, replaced by a jaded drunken old man's. "You're young and romantic, and you're the owner of a beautiful cock, Mr. Mills." She gave me a gentle squeeze between my legs. "Honor that cock. Don't wait for the second chance."

I remained silent, mortified for her and afraid of her all the same. Naïvely, I believed she was wrong—that life passes slowly, serving up chances every step of the way. But both happiness and misery are fleeting—longing and regret are all that remain—and I didn't know that then. I only knew I wanted her to stop. I drove my hands in the dark toward her breasts.

We fell asleep, scooped against each other, in the eerie early hours of the morning.

. . .

# ORIGAMI PRUNES

Laura and I spent the weekend in my apartment, going from bed to dryer—we discovered I could fit in as well, albeit tightly—to the kitchen, where we consoled our rapacious appetites with leftovers of week-old takeout and frozen pizza. Sunday was particularly noisy. I heard movement in the building, and also far away, down the street; the kind of sounds you hear when someone's moving in or out, mixed with a cacophony of sirens.

It was around midnight on Sunday when Laura approached the window, pulled the curtains open, and gasped.

"Mr. Mills!"

We hadn't watched TV or checked our phones in more than forty-eight hours. We'd disconnected ourselves from the world, and the world was reporting back to us. The Hill Country wildfires had reached the city, and the hills of Westlake, where Laura lived, were raging in the background, a hypnotic wave of burning drapes framing in orange the summer dark.

We turned on the TV. The wildfires trumped any story related to Michael Jackson's death, but the information was vague and chaotic. A mandatory evacuation of the city would be enforced the following morning. Military planes carrying evacuees were departing every few minutes. I asked Laura how I could help, make phone calls, get in touch with her family in Mexico or elsewhere, but she ignored me. She sat on the bed and stared vacantly through the window. I didn't know what to say.

"Please turn off the TV, and the lights," she asked. I closed the curtains and made to leave the room, but she waved me closer. She went back to bed and asked me to join her.

"We can't stay here, Laura. We have to go."

"I don't want to talk about that right now."

The sense of peace and separation from reality in the room

45

had vanished. The sirens howled like a mother lamenting the loss of her children; they had been all weekend, but now that I understood why, I could no longer ignore them. Laura snuggled next to me as if an endless summer of love still lay ahead, but the skin of her butt felt dry against my stomach, and our toes remained freezing cold, even after they tangled.

"Have you ever read José Emilio Pacheco, Mr. Mills?" Laura asked after a while.

"A little bit."

"Would you happen to know any of his poems by heart?"

"I don't, ma'am; I'm sorry. I vaguely remember a couple of lines; something I read in college."

"How do they go?"

"Let me see . . . There was one about how you only really meet the sea once in your life, and another that said, *When you turn forty / you become everything you despised / when you were twenty.* Something like that."

"Mr. Mills?"

"Yes, ma'am."

"Your phone."

I gave it to her, and she took one last picture of us—her back resting against my chest, both of us looking away. To this day, the image remains obscure and out of focus.


I fled Austin the next afternoon. The Mexican government provided a plane to evacuate the consulate personnel to Houston, where I spent the following weeks. Despite the efforts of firemen and the National Guard, the Hill Country wildfires swept through the city's ever-expanding limits. The state capital had to be temporarily reinstated in Houston. The consulate in Austin never reopened.

As compensation for our having lost everything, the Secretaría de Relaciones Exteriores offered to transfer us anywhere we liked. After visiting my parents in California, I moved to Paris, where I spent the next five years working for the embassy in the mornings, wandering the wobbly cobbled streets of the Rive Gauche and the Rive Droite and Place Vendôme and rue de Saint-Honoré and the Champs-Élysées in the afternoons, looking for Laura. I was later transferred to São Paulo, where I spent five miserable years, and then promoted to consul in Zürich, where my hopes of bumping into Laura on the street reached their lowest point, as I was sure she'd never pick such an aloof place. In all those years, I resisted the temptation to climb into a dryer again. In my fourth year, I learned about an opening in the Protection Department at the consulate in New York, an infamous middle-rank position that would force me to pretend once again that I cared. I wanted it regardless, because I wanted to be back in America.

Shortly after my arrival in Manhattan, an invitation to the opening of an exhibition by a Mexican artist at a SoHo gallery arrived in the consulate's in-box:

> *People Bleeding Firecrackers* is a series of 3D holograms
> in which Nicolasa Gutiérrez-Arteaga (Chimalistac, Mexico,
> 1991), recreates the cities where she was born and raised,
> Mexico City and Austin, Texas, as she blends them together
> into a single homeland, transient and elusive.

I recognized the name of the artist immediately. I looked her up online. When I found her picture, the hairs on my arms curled. The image showed a young woman whose features looked familiar. Her eyes were her mother's, but Nicolasa's looked unfathomably sad. It was like seeing a version of Laura's distorted by water and memory and make-believe. The invitation said the exhibition was to open in a couple of days, but I couldn't wait. I dashed out of my office and grabbed a taxicab.

The gallery was located on the grounds of a nineteenth century building with a cast-iron facade, overlooking a quiet, cobbled street. A young red-haired man greeted me ceremoniously at the door. Old-school manners were en vogue once again.

"Ms. Arteaga is not here at the moment, sir," he said, and my heart prickled. "May I ask who's looking for her?"

"Plutarco Mills. Mexican Consulate. Is she coming back today?"

"She is, indeed."

"Do you mind if I wait?"

"Not at all, sir," he said, looking startled. "Please make yourself at home." The gallery was a large white empty space flooded with bright light that didn't invite me to stay, but I didn't want to leave. I was anxious and filled with anticipation. I was convinced Laura would arrive any minute, trailing behind her now prominent daughter, playing her role of proud and submissive Mexican mother.

An hour later, a woman burst into the gallery, her arms full of shopping bags. It was her. The young man took the bags swiftly away from her, and whispered something in her ear. Nicolasa looked at me warily. The guy left us alone. As I approached her, I cleared my throat.

"Plutarco Mills, Mexican Consulate," I said, trying not to stammer as I offered Nicolasa my hand, my palm embarrassingly moist and shaky. "Very nice to meet you, Ms. Gutiérrez."

She was slender and tall, and wore an upsetting citrusy perfume I didn't recognize. She was dressed all in black. In person she wasn't nearly as beautiful or intriguing as her mother.

"It's actually Arteaga. Nice to meet you too," she said. I could tell she didn't mean the latter.

"I'm here to let you know that everybody at the consulate is very excited about the opening of your exhibition," I said in Spanish. Beads of sweat broke out on my scalp. "Anything we can do for you, just let me know. It will be my pleasure."

"Thank you. That's sweet of you," she replied, switching back to English, and this broke my heart. She offered me a diplomatic smile, but still looked unsettled. The word *sweet* a product of mere courtesy. I searched for echoes of Laura's fierceness, but I found none.

"It's funny," Nicolasa said, "I know some people at the consulate, but your name doesn't ring a bell."

"I'm new here," I replied. "I just moved back to the States after many years abroad. My last position in the country was with the Austin consulate."

"Really? I lived there for a while," Nicolasa revealed, as if I didn't know. Her face lit up. I imagined her mother back in Austin as I never had, shopping for groceries at H-E-B, driving the girls to soccer practice and art class and medical appointments and birthday parties, attending endless PTA meetings, picking her husband up at the airport, driving her Cayenne listlessly along Highway 360, all on her own, a world away from home, making stupid miles up and down a beautiful, meaningless place, looking for something, anything, that gave her a reason to keep on living. "It was my second home. Austin used to be such a gorgeous place."

I wanted to tell her I remembered the city the same, but her reasons and mine would have collided. I wanted her to repeat that word, *gorgeous*, for when she said it, she sounded like her mother.

*Gorgeous.*

"In fact, I think I met your parents there," I said. My stomach cramped. "How's your family doing?"

"Everybody's fine, thanks for asking." She looked unnerved. "They're flying in from Houston for the opening. I hope you join us, Mr. Mills." I knew she wanted me to leave, I knew she didn't mean to extend any invitation. I was scaring her, but she was forcing herself to say things she didn't mean out of pure Mexican-bred politeness. She was one of us, after all. I imagined Laura feeling proud of, and miserable for, her daughter's exquisite, self-destructive manners.

"I wouldn't miss it," I said, my voice trembling. I saw this pale, foreign girl in front of me, a complete stranger, and realized how absurd my presence there was, how disturbing and creepy my visit must have been to her. Excusing myself and leaving immediately was the right thing, the only thing, to do. But I couldn't help myself.

"I can't wait to see your mother again, Nicolasa," I heard myself say, as if the words had been uttered by somebody else. "After all these years, I haven't been able to forget her."

"My mother won't be here," Nicolasa replied quietly. "She died in the big Austin blaze of 2009."

"Oh," was all that came out of my mouth.

And then, as if she knew the right thing to say, she added, "I'm very sorry, Mr. Mills."


That last day I ever saw her, Laura woke me up with a whisper. It was very early in the morning.

She said she was leaving. I asked where she was going. She said she didn't know. I wanted to go with her, flee Austin together.

She said no.

She said she wanted to do this alone. I said we were a sphere, we were an elephant that had found its own lightness on the moon; we needed to remain a sphere.

She laughed as if she were a hundred years old, and her face darkened with sadness. She said she wished me luck, and that she hoped I would find someone who thrilled me.

I insisted, and she cupped my face in her hands. She came close to me, as if there were more people in the room.

"Goodbye, Mr. Mills," she breathed in my ear as if she were telling me a secret.

# I CLENCH MY HANDS INTO FISTS
# AND THEY LOOK LIKE SOMEONE ELSE'S

"Wait, Homero. Did you hear that?"

"Did I hear what?"

"That noise. Listen. There. In the kitchen."

"What does it sound like?"

"Like a scratch."

"Letting you try that shit was not a good idea, Ximena. It's frying your brain."

"I'm serious, Homero. There are *noises* in the apartment. *For real.*"

"I don't know what you're talking about, chimp."

"Wait. It stopped."

"Whatever."

"Anyway. You were saying—"

"Oh, yeah. Imagine yourself gliding for five hours straight. Imagine you could fly anywhere you want, free of everything and everybody, without having to worry about shit. Like, if you had wings."

"Like an eagle, all majestic and menacing? Or like a monarch butterfly? Frail and cute, but totally unbreakable?"

"Like an airplane. Like you had steel wings, but they were a natural part of your body."

"Whoa, dude. This shit's kind of scary."

"Like me."

"Yeah, you wish."

"Ximena?"

"What's up."

"What are those things on the curtains?"

"Those cute little bugs printed all over them? The blue ones look like flies, no? And the other ones—aren't they like, ladybugs?"

"That's gross. And *super* gay. Who'd put curtains with *bugs* in their *living* room?"

"They're kinda cool."

"You don't have to like *everything* just 'cause we're here, Ximena. We're not offending Philippe by not liking his apartment. He can't hear us, you know? They're *awful*."

"I'm just trying to like *something* about this place, okay?"

"Don't look at the windows, then. Those curtains are ugly as shit."

"Homero?"

"What now?"

"Remember that time we all came to New York?"

"For Christmas?"

"Where did we have dinner?"

"At the Plaza, I think. Or the Waldorf. One of those places near Central Park."

"When Mom and Dad said we could stay in Philippe's apartment, I imagined something like that, around the park, with a doorman and everything. Not *this*."

"At least we're not in Harlem, chimp. Or *Brooklyn*."

"Did Grandma and Grandpa come with us on that trip?"

"Oh, yeah. On Christmas Eve, Grandpa took you, me, Nico, and Fer to FAO Schwarz while everybody else got ready for dinner. He bought us Tamagotchis. Mom and Aunt Laura were so pissed, but Grandma told them to chill, like she always did."

"I barely remember Grandma."

"You were too young, chimp."

"Do you think she's looking?"

"*From above?*"

"Uh-huh."

"Nah. Better for her, though."

"Why do you say that?"

"'Cause it would kill her again—knowing about Grandpa."

"Homero?"

"Yes, chimp."

"There's this *girl thing* I used to talk about with Carla and Michelle?"

"If it's what I'm thinking, don't even go there."

"Just got it today. And it's like, *alive*, man."

"TMI, dude."

"Who am I supposed to talk to about these things now?"

"Not to me. That's *gross*. Talk to Mom when she calls."

"Are you out of your mind? 'Hey, Mom! Guess what? I've got my period! Five days late. Isn't that *a relief?*' "

"Ximena, stop. I mean it."

"Easy for you to say. You guys fool around and everything's cool. We girls mess around a little bit, and we're screwed. It's depressing. And unfair."

"Maybe, but I'm not fucking Doctor Ruth, okay? Read my lips: T.M.I."

"How old are you? Nine? 'Mo-om, Ximena said the word *va-gi-na* in front of me!'"

"Fuck you, chimp."

"No, Homero! Fuck *you!*"


"Homero?"

"Not here, dude."

"It's that noise again. Did you hear it?"

"It's those ladybugs and flies. They're coming for you, chimp."

"Shut up, Homero. I'm serious."

"Forget it, smarty pimples. Not talking to you unless you apologize."

"Don't be a dick."

"Good luck finding someone to listen to your shit here. Not talking to a young lady from Virreyes who behaves like a truck driver from Neza."

"Hey, you said *fuck you* first!"

"Remember what Mom and Dad said at the airport?"

"What part? They said, 'Look out for each other. You guys will be on your own until we can join you.' They said, 'Don't get in trouble. We have enough of that already.'"

"And they said, 'Homero, you're in charge.'"

"They never said that!"

"Of course they did! They *always* do. And even if they

didn't, it was *implicit*. I'm *older*, chimp. I'm the fucking boss around here. So, *apologize* or else."

"Seriously, dude. You're such a douche."

"That noise is totally freaking me out, Homero. Can't believe you don't hear it."

"Apparently it's douche-proof, 'cause I can't hear a damn thing."

"Fine. I'm sorry, okay? Can we keep talking now?"

"Not so fast, smarty freckles. First you need to say, 'I'm sorry, Homero, my irresistibly hot, and wise as hell, older brother. I was a bad and stupid girl. I hereby admit you'll be in charge for as long as we're stuck here.'"

"Give me a break, seriously. My head's throbbing like crazy."

"My head feels watermelon-huge too."

"I told you. Popping pills you find in the bathroom cabinet of someone you barely know is probably not the brightest of ideas. But you said that it'd be a riot. So much for your being in charge, dude."

"I'm pretty sure we'd have a headache anyways, even if we'd only be doing fucking *Pop-Tarts*. It's not the pills, Ximena. It's that we're stuck in *limbo*."

"Did you hear that? Don't tell me you didn't."

"You're getting on my nerves, chimp. What if I didn't hear a fucking thing?"

"No wonder."

"No wonder what?"

"No wonder you're still single, dude. You're unbearable."

"You sound like Grandpa."

57

"Excuse me?"

"Every time I saw him, he'd put his arm around my shoulder like we were buddies, and ask the same fucking thing over and over: 'Have you got yourself a girlfriend yet, Hom? How come I've never met a girlfriend of yours?'"

"Homero?"

"Ugh. What?"

"Do you like dudes?"

"Note to self: stop treating your fifteen-year-old sister as if she had a brain."

"So? Do you like girls then? Yes or no."

"I used to, till I had to share a shitty apartment in New York with one. Didn't I tell you about her? She wouldn't shut up, *caw caw caw caw caw* like a fucking parrot all day. And she *heard noises*. Totally cuckoo. Born-again faggot ever since, dude."

"Ha. Ha. Ha. You're so hilarious I'm peeing in my undies."

"Just keepin' it real, Sis."

"You don't want to talk about yourself? Fine. I've got a question for you, though."

"Here we go again. Wake me up when you're at least twenty, please."

"Do you think it's possible to like guys but like, dislike having sex with them?"

"Absolutely, chimp. That fleshy thingy dangling in between dudes' legs? Gross."

"Every time I try to talk about something serious with you, you make fun of me."

"Let's pretend we didn't have this conversation *at all*, chimp. You're too young to worry about that dude shit yet."

"Thanks for the advice, *Dad*! God, that was so fucking sissy now I'm *positive* you *love* dudes. Big time. Like, dudes with *huge* cocks, man."

"Can we keep talking about wings?"

"Really? That's so two hours ago."

"Come on, Homero. I'm getting claustrophobic in here. I need a break."

"Where did we leave off?"

"You were saying you wish you had steel wings."

"Just wings, all right? Real wings, any way you like."

"Fly-away wings."

"Exactly! See-ya-Mexico-and-all-your-shit wings. I'm-leaving-for-real wings."

"Homesick wings. I-miss-my-friends-and-my-life wings. I-hate-this-lousy-apartment wings. I-hate-New-York-so-much-it's-painful wings. I-so-wanted-to-live-here-one-day wings."

"Careful-what-you-wish-for wings."

"I-wanna-go-home wings."

"Good-luck-with-that wings."

"Shut-up wings. We're-going-back wings."

"We're-so-not wings. If-they-don't-hear-about-Grandpa-soon-we're-so-sticking-around-here wings."

"Is-there-something-you-know-that-I-don't wings?"

"Swear to God there isn't. *Wings*."

"God's so fucking last month. *Wings*. What do you know?"

"Nothing. I'm serious. And enough with the *f word*, chimp. You sound cheap."

"And you don't?"

"I sound *badass*. *You* sound cheap. Guys don't like girls who talk like that."

"What makes you think I want guys to like me?"

. . .

"Tell me, Homero. Whatever it is, I want to know."

"I'm serious, chimp. I don't know anything. It's just a bad feeling, okay? But you'll laugh if I tell you about it."

"No, I won't, Homero. I promise. Seriously."

"I'm having visions about Grandpa. That's all."

"What kind of visions?"

"It's like, I see him at the end of a street, in a sea of people. He's traipsing around as if he doesn't know which way to go. I feel so relieved when I see him cause I think, 'Oh, that was *it*! He was just *lost*!' I grow all excited because *I've found him*, you know? I'm going to rescue him, to bring him home. I tap him on the shoulder, but when he turns . . ."

"What?"

"His whole face, Ximena."

"What's wrong with it?"

"He's got no eyes. No ears. No tongue."

"Homero, it's not real. It's just a *vision*. I'm sure Grandpa is okay."

"No, he's not."

"How can you be so sure?"

"'Cause I feel it."

"Don't say that. He'll be fine, you'll see. They'll get him back, and he'll be *fucking fantastic*. And we'll go home. Believe me. Let's both believe it, so that it *will* happen, okay?"

"I wish I could be like you, chimp."

"Why's that?"

"I wish I still believed in shit."

"You can be really mean when you want to, Homero. Seriously."

"I'm not messing with you. I totally mean it."

. . .

"It's there again, Homero!"

"It's just your brain turning into a french fry, chimp. No more pills for you, lady."

"Seriously, Homero. I've been hearing that fucking noise in the kitchen since we arrived, and you keep saying it's all in my head. You're scaring the shit out of me. You're–"

"It's okay, Ximena. I was just being a dick. Seriously."

"Are you serious? Tell me you are, please."

"I am. I'm sorry, okay? Stop crying."

"Do you think it could be mice?"

"Or rats. They say there are more rats than people in New York."

"Thanks for sharing that, man. Now I won't be able to sleep here *ever again*."

"Or maybe it's just the walls, the floor, creaking, crumbling, you know? This fucking building's like, a thousand years old."

"No, it's not that. Sounds like something alive."

"I need to go out, Homero. I need some air."

"Where are you going?"

"I don't know. Shopping. Out for a walk."

"Can you grab something to eat on the way back?"

"Why don't you come with me? Let's have dinner out. We need to get out of here. We can go shopping together. It'll be fun!"

"Shopping with you? I'd rather stay here and be eaten by rats."

"Come on. Let's go. You've hardly gone out since we got here."

"Thanks, though, but I don't feel like going out. It depresses me."

61

"What are you talking about? We're in fucking Manhattan, man!"

"We could be in fucking Mars and it still would."

"Brought you Chipotle. The other places I checked out looked gross."

"Thanks, chimp."

"I met our neighbor from the apartment next door, she came in at the same time."

"Fascinating."

"She's like, two hundred years old, but nice and petite and like, elegant? She said she lives alone. She said it's rats."

"Beg your pardon?"

"The scratching noises that we've been hearing. She actually brought it up. She said she hears them too because our kitchen and hers share the same wall. She said she was pretty sure the rats were on *our* side. She said they've tried everything, but that they always come back."

"I guess we'll be eating Chipotle for a while then."

"She suggested that we get some special traps, and something else; something *supercreepy*."

"What did she say?"

"She said we need to get a good *snap trap* and use blue cheese as bait. She said, 'Those little guys love the good stuff.' She said the trap would catch the rat by its head and hopefully kill it instantly. Then, she advised, 'Release it from the trap and stab it in the belly with a meat fork, but do it *good*, two or three times if you can, my dear, as if you were going mad all over it, and then leave the little guy there, with the meat fork in its belly and everything. Don't move it, don't clean any of the mess. It won't look pretty, my dear, let me tell you. It'll start smelling funny after a couple days, and you'll want to get rid of it, but you'll have to hang in there, you've got to *leave it there,*' she said. You should've seen her face, Homero, all calm and sweet and yet talking like she was in fucking *Kill Bill* or something. I couldn't believe my ears, I was getting sick, I couldn't move. I wasn't even sure the whole fucking thing was real, if it wasn't my fried brain getting all worked up."

"That's a possibility, but anyway. What else did she say? *Supposedly.*"

"She said, 'One day, you'll come to the kitchen and find out the little guy's body is gone. Perhaps you'll find the meat fork tossed aside, or you won't. But it'll have disappeared. Don't ask me to explain how it happens, my dear, because I can't. I can only tell you *it works.* After that you won't hear more noises for a couple months."

"That wasn't an old lady. That was a *fucking ninja.*"

"Swear to God I'm not making it up, Homero. After that she jotted down the brand of traps on a scrap of paper and handed it to me. Here. Look."

"That's awesome. Anyway, I'm not setting up any fucking *Tomcat snap trap* or stabbing anything any time soon."

"That's what I told her."

"And what did she say?"

"She whispered, as if we were part of some plot, 'I know that the idea of harming those little guys sounds revolting, my dear. It was hard for me to bring myself to do it the first time. I mean, *me* killing a poor creature! I donate to PETA! I'm against animal testing! Dogfighting! Bullfighting! Starbucks! Republicans! But I had no choice. It was either me or them. If one of those fellas gets its way with you, you'll be in trouble. They are rabid and heartless, to say the least. Take my advice, my dear. You don't want to end up in some lousy ER in Lower Manhattan just because you took mercy on one of those nasty creatures, especially *in your situation*, do you?'"

"What did she mean by that?"

"Who the hell knows!"

"Didn't you ask?"

"How could I? I was speechless, Homero! I was just trying to grasp the whole fucking thing!"

"How did you like the tacos?"

"They were disgusting. But I guess I'd better get used to them."

"I know. Food sucks. *Here*, of all places."

"Mom called while you were out, by the way."

"Really?"

"No, not really. I just made it up for fucking shit's sake. Look at the phone."

"What did she say?"

"That she's been checking out the credit card, and that you've got to stop."

"Yeah, right."

"Not kidding you, dude. She said we need to start being cautious with money 'cause she didn't know how much longer we'd need to stay here. That's the word she used. *Cautious*."

"That's nonsense. Why would she say that?"

"'Cause the shit hit the fan big-time? I told you, chimp. She said she and Dad are coming over, probably as soon as next week. I asked if we were all going home right after, and she said no. She said that they were looking for a place for the four of us to stay, that they were checking out houses online in Connecticut, 'cause it's cheaper than the city."

"You're fucking kidding me."

"Am I fucking laughing?"

. . .

"What about Grandpa? Did she say anything about him?"

"No."

"Did you ask her?"

"What do you think?"

"So?"

"She changed the subject. She wanted to know how we were liking the apartment. She said Philippe had told them we'd love its *shabby-chic-ness*. Go fucking figure."

"Did you tell her it's a fucking *shabby-chic mess*?"

"Seriously, dude, no more pills for you. That shit's dumbing you down. Grandpa's probably dead already. God only knows what's going on at home. Do you really think Mom and Dad could give a fuck about this filthy joint right now? We're not going back, Ximena! We're staying here *for good*! Do you fucking get it? Do you?"

"Don't yell at me."

"Then stop talking like someone squeezed your stupid brain up your fucking fat ass, moron!"

"You're not the only one freaking out, okay?"

"But I seem to be the only one still trying to think straight."

"Your problem is that you're so scared you're probably peeing in your pants right now, but you'll never admit it."

"And what's your problem with that?"

"That I'm here too. And you're making me feel lonely as shit."

"Are you sure we'll be fine? That last headache was a bitch, man."

"Yeah, I've tried these before. We'll be good."

"I don't know why I still trust you."

. . .

"You there, chimp?"

"Here. What."

"One day, we'll go back to the past, you know?"

"How's that?"

"Everything will be like it used to be. Not like, a month ago, but *way* back. Back to how it should have been in the first place. Ancient and natural and . . . *correct*."

"We'll be so doomed by then. We'll be history, dude. We'll be done already."

"Nah, we'll still be around. It'll happen sooner than you think. Everybody will be like, '*What the fuck?*' and no one will be able to make sense of any of it. *No one* will be able to explain how it happened, and everybody will be so fucking scared they will all want to shit in their pants. But they won't."

"Why not?"

"'Cause we'll be there to say, '*Chill*. It's okay to be afraid. We'll be fine.'"

"Ximena?"

"Uh-huh."

"What is it about guys that freaks you out?"

"Like you really want to know."

"Fine. But then don't come to me complaining that I don't listen to your shit."

"Dicks. Just their dicks, okay?"

"What about them?"

"Carla and Michelle and everybody else are now totally into them, as though they were *collecting* them. I didn't want to feel left out."

"Got it. So you went and had some. And . . ."

66

"It was gross."

"What about boobs?"

"I'm not a lesbian, asshole, if that's what you're trying to say."

"Wouldn't be the end of the world. What's the problem with liking boobs?"

"That I really wanted to like guys."

"Does Grandpa really ask you about girls all the time?"

"He's *relentless*."

"That's gross."

"Remember the time he made a business trip to São Paulo over spring break and I went with him?"

"Uh-huh."

"One night, after dinner, his colleagues went to a nightclub. Grandpa said he was tired, but that I should go. I said okay, thinking that we'd just have caipirinhas, dance samba with beautiful garotas, you know? We got to the club, and a woman at the entrance asked if I was going to get *full service*. Before I could answer, one of his colleagues said that I was, and paid for me. I looked at him, all confused. He just patted me on the back and said, 'Don't worry, son. Your old man asked me to take care of you.'"

"Oh. My. God."

"A girl picked me up at the table and took me to a private room. I kind of wanted to like it, you know? But when she got naked and started to do her thing, I felt so uncomfortable and *disgusted*, I thought I was going to barf. I told her that I wasn't really in the mood, and asked if she didn't mind that we stayed there for a while so everybody would think we had a good time."

. . .

"Homero?"

"Yes, chimp."

"Do you know how much I admire you?"

"You're high, dude. Try to get some sleep."

"Homero?"

"Uh-oh. She's still alive. Those damn pills didn't work after all."

"What part of your body do you like the most?"

"Whoa. She's alive *and* asking brilliant questions. My fists, I guess."

"Really? Why?"

"I don't know. I clench my hands into fists and they look like someone else's. You?"

"They're there. The rats. Do you hear them?"

"Yeah, I do. Answer me."

"Let me think of a *feminine* version of your fists. *My earlobes*?"

"Does it hurt, to pierce your ears?"

"Only if you think about it."

"Those fucking rats are there again, Homero. What are we gonna do about them?"

"There's nothing we can do about them, chimp."

"Shouldn't we try *something*?"

"We should get wings. We should get a couple tattoos at one of those parlors on St. Mark's. Something *sick*. Mom and Dad will freak out. They'll think we've become fucking Maras when they see us."

"It's not funny, Homero. What if the neighbor was right? What if those fucking rats find their way through, and get to us? Are we just gonna sit here and do *nothing*? I'm serious, man."

"I am too. We're taking over Manhattan, chimp, like the *fucking* Muppets. Those pussy rats are getting owned. We're getting tattoos. Tomorrow, first thing in the morning. Big ones. Across our backs. A fucking thousand badass wings sticking out of our spines, reaching for the goddamn sky."

# DEERS

When I got to work that morning there were a bunch of police cars and fire trucks and vans from TV outside the McDonald's, and my shift mates were there too, behind a yellow tape that read AUSTIN POLICE DEPARTMENT DO NOT TRESPASS, trying to get a peek of what was going on inside, including Conchita; she was on her toes because she was short like me, and when I tapped on her shoulder she turned and shrieked, "Susy girl!" and we hugged real tight, and she said, "Susy girl, you're not gonna believe what's happening inside," and I said, "Conchita, what's going on?" really worried because, you know, when I saw those police cars, those cops around, I thought, This can't be good, this is trouble, I started thinking, I probably should go home and start looking for another job, but Conchita already knew how to read me; she already knew about my fears so she looked into my eyes, grabbed my arm, and whispered, "Relax, Susy girl, it's not what you're thinking," and I just smiled, still nervous, though, because I get nervous every time cops are around, but also relieved because I trusted Conchita and I knew that if she said, "Relax," I could, things would be okay; she'd earned my trust a few months before, the day there was a raid at my apartment complex and Conchita heard about it on the radio on her way to work, and when she saw me walk into the restaurant the next day she ran to me and hugged me tight and stroked my hair like she was my mother or something, and whispered in my ear, "I was so worried for you, Susy girl," and she looked so relieved that it got me thinking, One of these days I'll run out of luck and perhaps Conchita won't see me come to work the next day, and then I thought of my little ones, my Pedro and my Santiago and my Adrián, I wondered who'd call them back in Cuévano to let them know their mother had been arrested, perhaps Conchita would but I didn't know how she could because she wouldn't know what number to call, and the next time I saw Conchita I gave her the number of my mother's house, but she said, "Don't be silly, Susy girl, you've got more lives than a cat!" and hugged me tight, and it felt good, not only that we hugged but that I had someone to trust; so this time around I whispered in her ear, "If it's nothing bad, then what's with all these cops and all these fire trucks and the whole thing?" and Conchita giggled hard, she got this funny face, I didn't know if she was going to cry or laugh or what; you know that face; imagine if the Virgin Mary showed up like, Bam! out of the blue in front of you, and you were like, Whoa! but also like, Wow! and, Yikes!, all at the same time; that was the face Conchita got, and then she said, "They say there's a bear inside the place, Susy girl!" and she got real funny now, she stopped talking but her eyes kept shining and this reminded me of my Pedro and my Santiago and my Adrián; I remembered their faces when they were younger, before I had to leave Mexico City with Doña Laura and her family, when I'd visit them on my weekends off with cotton candy and chocolate bars that I'd buy at the bus terminal in Mexico City, they'd be waiting for me by the road because they missed me, I hope, but also because they knew I always had something sweet for them, and so I'd step off the bus with three cotton candies like a bouquet of hydrangeas in my hand, and there they'd be, all groomed by my mother, smelling fresh and clean like they were babies again, shining from head to toe, beaming like waterfalls, ready to kiss me and get their mouths sticky and full of sugar, but anyway; Conchita stood there, looking deep into my eyes with this funny and serious and silly and shiny face, explaining that a bear had taken over the McDonald's where we worked; she said it like it was for real but I couldn't help feeling she was kidding me, so I waited a couple seconds for her to say something else but she didn't; meanwhile the noises grew louder and louder around us, sirens of fire trucks and patrol cars howling and police talking on walkie-talkies and mobs of onlookers gossiping about this bear everybody insisted was inside; they were trying to guess where he'd come from, and one of them said he heard a circus was in town; "What if he's a runaway circus slave who has decided to stop putting on the same show every night?" he said; somebody else said the bear could have come from one of the big houses nearby; "Yeah, one of those huge mansions up in the hills, rich people are just getting richer," somebody else said, "and you know what happens when people lose track of how much they have, they start doing crazy things like keeping bears as pets," he said, which made me imagine the bear caged inside a big house, like the one where I lived with Doña Laura and her family for a few months until one day, out of the blue, she got mad and kicked me out; I imagined the bear alone, forced to live in a strange place surrounded only by humans; I wondered if this was a young or an old bear, if he missed the company of other bears or if bears didn't have those feelings, if they were lucky in that way; "What if he's not a bear but a coyote or a mountain lion?" somebody else said, "people are so ignorant about animals these days, especially if they went to public schools," he said; "Hey, what's wrong with public education?" someone else replied, "If you think like that then you're part of the problem!" she said; the onlookers were saying all these things I didn't understand, they remained outside the restaurant and wouldn't leave, like the rest of us, but unlike them, we did have a reason to be there because we worked there; they just wanted to spot the bear like it was Brad Pitt or Enrique Iglesias so they could go crazy all over him, ask for an autograph, take a picture with him, and Conchita didn't speak for so long I started to feel something was off with her, because when everything around us was loud and unbearable, silence would bring us peace; that we knew from experience, because a few months back, weeks after that raid at my complex, Conchita didn't come to work for a few days and when she finally showed up she looked like a tractor had run her over, and when she arrived we only had time to hug but not to talk, so I looked for her at lunch break and asked her, "Conchita, what happened? Are you all right?" and she stayed there, leaning against the storage door like her mind was somewhere else, her silence longer than Lent, and I thought she didn't want to talk so I turned to leave but then she mumbled, "Don't go, Susy girl, please," and when I turned back she told me what had happened to Jonathan, her youngest, the one she called Jon; how she and her family had gone out for a picnic by the Colorado River on Saturday and she'd told the kids, "Don't go in the river because the water is traicionera!" but they wouldn't listen, "They never listen to me," Conchita said, and the family was alone when Jon went under and they didn't want to call 911 even though they could, because that was always a prob-

lem, "Police see you moreno and dressed like my kids do, and
they only think ganga, they only think mojados, they start asking silly questions instead of moving their asses to help you
out," Conchita said, and when they finally called 911 the
police couldn't find him, they looked for Jon through the
night, they kept looking for him the next day, Sunday, and on
Monday and Tuesday too; and Conchita's last words to him
were, "Don't go in the water! Jon! Jon! Are you sordo o qué?
Güerco malcriado, come back here!" but she didn't have a
chance to say goodbye, she didn't give him a hug or bury him
because Jon's body was never found, and she told me all this
really fast, like she had to tell it ra-ta-ta-ta-ta or else she couldn't,
and after she said all that she stayed there, quietly by the storage door, and I did too, our mouths shut; then I opened my
arms and she let herself go like Jesus falling off the cross; I
wrapped her in the tightest hug, her body heavy in my arms,
and we remained like that for a while until lunch break was
over and the manager came by and nagged us to go back to
work; so this time around I thought something similar was
going on with Conchita and that was why she wasn't talking,
but curiosity was killing me already; I wanted to know more
about this bear, so I said, "What do you mean there's a bear
inside the place, Conchita?" and she replied, "I swear to God
they say it's a bear, Susy girl! A real bear, like Yogi Bear, you
know?" and I said, "I don't know what you're talking about,
Conchita," and she said, "You must've seen that show, Susy
girl! Yogi Bear, remember? A bear that lives in a national park
in California and he's a *real* bear, and he's real nice and goofy,
and he wears a hat and a tie, and he goes nuts craving picnic
meals all the time? Don't tell me you didn't see that show,
Susy girl!" and I got dizzy because I had no idea what she was
talking about and I didn't know what craving meant exactly

either; I'd just came from Mexico with Doña Laura and her family the year before and English was a nightmare to learn; every time people would say something I didn't get, I'd feel embarrassed to admit I had no clue, I felt like my head was gonna explode, but Conchita had helped me a lot already, she'd been real sweet to me, so I let go; "Sorry, Conchita, but it's the first time in my life I've heard about that bear," I said, and she looked at me like I was kidding her; "C'mon, Susy girl, everybody, *everybody*, knows Yogi!" and I said, "Well, I guess that's here, but back in Cuévano we didn't have that show, you know, our TV at home had only one channel and we just watched soap operas and *La Carabina de Ambrosio* and *Chabelo* and *Siempre en Domingo* but no shows with bears; ask me anything about actresses and singers, Gina Montes, Verónica Castro, Victoria Ruffo, or Carmen Montejo if you like, but don't ask me about goofy bears that wear hats," I said, and Conchita cracked up like what I'd just said was a good joke; I felt that every time I said something dumb I made her laugh; I felt that that was the reason she liked to call me Susy girl; like she knew I found shelter in the tone of her voice, especially if she had to explain something the manager had said in a meeting, because the manager, oh God; he'd speak so fast, he'd barely open his mouth and I wouldn't get what he said most of the time; Conchita would only need to look at my face, she'd crack up and whisper in my ear, "Don't worry, Susy girl, I'll explain it to you later," and so Conchita did it again this time; "Okay, let's start from scratch, Susy girl, forget what I said about Yogi, okay? They say there's a real bear inside the place, a real grizzly bear! Apparently he's big and hungry as hell, because I heard that when the cops got here they spotted him in the back, by the storage, you know, eating all the English muffins we left on the trays ready for the morning rush? Apparently this big fella was eating them all with the wrappers and everything! They said that he also tried to break into the freezer and tried to drink from the soda fountain machines! I mean, the guy's a *real* bear and is all over our place! Isn't that like, a miracle?" and she started laughing like she was losing it, making no sense at all, and I didn't know what to make of what she'd just said; meanwhile the number of people around us was growing, everybody kept on pushing and pushing against the metal barrier installed by the police to keep us at bay, trying to get a better view of the restaurant, but the lights inside were out and the cops and firemen weren't doing anything; they stayed still, talking on their walkie-talkies without making a move, which made me think that maybe all of it was bullshit, or that they didn't know how to deal with him, that maybe they were waiting for him to finish off the food and leave on his own will, or maybe they were afraid of him, or maybe there was no bear at all, maybe it was just a rumor somebody had made up and everybody wanted it to be real; I didn't know, but I'd never seen so many cops in my life and I was starting to feel scared, the whole thing was loud and messy like a Holy Week procession that was getting bigger and bigger and bigger; then a group of young people with signs that read DON'T SHOOT THE BEAR, GIVE BEARS A CHANCE, DO I LOOK ILLEGAL?, SAY YES TO LIFE NO TO JUNK FOOD, PUT YOUR PAWS UP, showed up and started chanting slogans and then there we were, Conchita and the rest of my shift mates and me; we should have already been working inside, serving breakfast, handing bags of muffins with omelette and sausage or whatever people would order through the drive-through, and I should've already cleaned up the bathrooms because the first thing I had to do every morning was make sure they were all beaming, as the manager would always find time to go in there and check if I'd cleaned them up, and every morning Conchita would also find the time to stop by and say hello and give me a hug; "Ay, Susy girl!" she'd say and explain that it was one of the downsides of working at McDonald's on the west side of town, because on the east side, she'd say, "Those joints by Riverside or way south down Airport Boulevard, managers there don't give a damn if bathrooms are filthy as a cockroach butt," she'd say, "but here customers make a fuss if they spot a dust bunny by the sink, they make a fuss out of everything, like this is freaking Whole Foods," she'd say, and I thought about all that while looking at her outside the restaurant; I remembered how funny and strong and confident Conchita was before, how much she'd changed since Jon died; now she was just staring at me like she didn't have anything else to say; "Conchita, you're kidding me, there are no bears in Austin, I've seen vultures and deers but no bears," I said but she cut me off, "Deer," she said, "What?" I said, "Deer, Susy girl, you don't say deers, you say deer," and I said, "No, Conchita, deers, *many*, there are lots of them around here, especially in the evening; haven't you seen them at the end of the day, while we're waiting for the bus? They come by the avenue in packs, like little families; deers of all sizes; some are really big and kind of intimidating, with antlers and everything, but some are small; they look tender and vulnerable like newborns, covered with white spots, like freckles," I said but Conchita insisted, "I know, Susy girl, there are lots of them around here but you always call them deer, whether it's one or a bunch," and I said, "Why?" "What do I know, Susy girl? I didn't invent the language, I'm not freaking Shakespeare, you know?" Conchita said, and I just couldn't get my head around it; "You're making me dizzy, Conchita, if I tell you I saw deer on my way here, how do you know if I saw one or four?" I asked, and Conchita looked at me like I was in first grade; "I don't know, Susy girl, that's a good question," she said and looked down with a frown, like she'd never thought about it before; "That's the kind of questions Jon asked all the time, you know, he'd just come up with these questions that were hard," she said; "Anyway, Conchita," I said because I didn't want her to get depressed again, especially not after some stupid question that I'd asked; "There are no bears around here, so how come there's a bear inside the restaurant eating our muffins? That's just off," I said; "Exactly, Susy girl! That's my point! Doesn't it sound like something out of a blessing? Of all the McDonald's in the world, why would he choose ours? There has to be a reason for that, Susy girl, and a higher one at that!" she said cheerfully again, like she'd already forgotten what we were talking about a minute ago and I felt relieved, so I said, "Is it like a miracle then?" pretending to follow her; "Right! It's like an apparition!" she cheered; "Why not?" I went on, and we giggled together; "We need to find a way to see him! We can't miss this chance, Susy girl!" Conchita said, and so we were talking about miracles and apparitions and stuff like that when the manager showed up and called out to us; he told us to walk behind the restaurant because he needed to talk with us, and the police let us slip under the yellow tape, and when one of them pulled it up so I could pass, I felt a shiver; a cold sweat running down my spine and from the tip of my nose to my pinkies and my fingernails, but nothing happened; the cop ignored me; he didn't notice anything different on my face or my smell or anything; the back parking lot had been cordoned too, it was empty and less noisy than the front and it even felt calm; there were no police cars, no fire trucks, no TV cameras, no onlookers, no protesters, only the fifteen of us, who gathered around the manager like when we'd meet at the beginning of a shift by the frying machines; he didn't say hello or good morning or, "Boy, what a crazy day," nothing, curt and distant as always; he reminded me of Doña Laura the last days I lived in her house, she'd wake up in a bad mood every morning; "So, a goddamn bear that came out of nowhere invaded our workplace under circumstances that remain unclear at this point," he spat, like he hadn't seen the bear himself but he already hated him bad, like he could already picture himself being transferred to another branch on East Austin for having let this happen; "Police are still trying to find those who might be responsible for this, but that's not the point; the point is, they don't know what the hell to do with it yet, because simply shooting the damn thing, as much as I'd like that, is not an option for various reasons," he said, tapping the asphalt with his left foot; he was a short, stocky, gray-haired man who would always wear these supershiny ugly brown moccasins; he'd wear the same pair to work every day, and I imagined him waking up early every morning to polish those hideous shoes like nothing else mattered; "So, since I don't have a time line for this goddamn mess to be solved," he was saying when Conchita cut him off, "I have a question; are they gonna let us see him?" she said, and the manager glared at her and barked, "What did you say?" and I thought, Oh boy, not again; I felt the guy was finally gonna snap because in the weeks after Jon died he and Conchita would fight every day; Conchita would ask him questions that put him on edge during the morning meetings, or she'd yell back at him if he gave her an order she didn't like or pointed out that she was performing her duties "in a careless manner," and other employees began to whisper that Conchita's days were numbered and that the only reason she hadn't gotten the boot yet was because the manager didn't have the balls to fire a middle-aged woman who'd recently lost a child, which made me feel anxious and frail; I imagined myself alone at the meetings without Conchita, struggling to understand a thing; "The bear!" she yelled at him, "What's with it?" he cried back, "Are they gonna let us see the bear?" Conchita said; her voice broke in the middle of the sentence and I realized she was crying; my guts turned into a knot because I wanted to help her, but I couldn't; I wished that she'd stop because I didn't want the manager to fire her right there, but Conchita wouldn't back down; "You have to do something about it! You're the boss here; don't you see this is a chance we'll never get again? Ask them to let us see him!"; she yelled like it was an order; the tension felt like a piece of meat, heavy in the air, and I was sure everybody was thinking, This is it, Conchita will never french-fry another potato here again, and I closed my eyes wanting for the whole ordeal to stop; the noises from the front of the restaurant reached my ears again, growing louder inside my head, and I heard the walkie-talkies and the sirens and the live reports and the chants, GIVE BEARS A CHANCE! GIVE BEARS A CHANCE! again and again, but I also heard Conchita's lungs, her hard breathing and her sobbing, very loud and close to me like my ears were pressed against her chest; "So?" she howled, "Are you gonna do something about it?" I opened my eyes and looked at the manager, but he wouldn't say anything; I looked at his ugly moccasins first and then at his khaki pants and then at his white crisp shirt and then at his red face; his mouth was now shut and his eyes were watery, like it had just hit him, like he'd just realized why Conchita had gone bananas, but she wouldn't shut up; "Can you please ask them to let us see him at least once?" she implored, and everybody's eyes were on him, and he seemed small and flimsy; it was the first and only time I felt sorry for him, and when I did

I surprised myself because I never imagined myself feeling sorry for someone I was so afraid of, I never felt for Doña Laura what I was feeling for this man right there, not even when I knew what had happened to her father; I imagined the manager alone at home, polishing his ugly shoes by the bed, wondering why no one loved him yet; "I'm sorry, Concepción, I don't think that would be possible at all," he replied in a sorrowful voice that revealed he was human after all, a horrible one, but human nonetheless; "Okay," was all Conchita said and covered her face with her small hands, with her chubby fingers full of silver rings, her sobbing sounded muffled and unstoppable; "Anyway," the manager said after clearing his throat, "Corporate called to say it's better for everybody to stay out of the picture, so you have to go, you're all off the hook; it will count as a comp day," he said and rolled his eyes, like he was the same old asshole again; "Just one more thing before you all leave," he said menacingly, "talking to the media is strictly prohibited, or else you'll be let go;" the rest of my shift mates made off toward the front parking lot but the manager called out again; "What part of *you have to go* didn't you understand? You're not allowed to stay and watch! This is not a goddamn show! Is that clear?" he yelled, but I stayed at the back by Conchita's side; I looked in my purse and handed her a Kleenex, and as she blew her nose, I stroked her hair; "So, what do we do now?" I asked her to see if that cheered her up, "What are we supposed to do now, Conchita? I didn't get what he said," I lied; "You know what?" she said after she stopped sobbing and cleaned up the washed-out mascara around her eyes, "Let's have some fun today, Susy girl, the day is ours! When was the last time you or me had the entire day only for us? Let's go to the mall or the movies or whatever! How about that?" she said, making an effort to smile, and I thought that it

would do us both good because she was right, but I also thought I'd never gone to the movies in Austin and I didn't know how much it cost; I worried it would be expensive and I was in no position to spend money on silly things; I needed to send all I could back home, and that's when I thought of my Pedro and my Santiago and my Adrián again; I tried to remember the last time we watched a movie together, and I couldn't; I tried to imagine how much they'd have changed since I left them behind in Cuévano with my mother, and I couldn't; "I'd love to, Conchita, but I'm not sure, you know my budget's tight and I probably should—" I was saying when Conchita cut me off, "Shhh! Do you hear that?" she said, "What?" I said, "That noise," she said, "Don't you hear it?" We stayed in silence and then I did, the noise seemed to come from inside the restaurant, slipping through the bottom of the back door, just a few yards away from where we were; it was a soft thrashing sound, like the sound you'd make tearing apart a plastic bag; "I do!" I whispered excitedly; "It's him!" Conchita cheered quietly, her eyes filled with life again, like she was announcing that Jesus had arrived; "You think so?" I whispered; "C'mon, Susy girl, we can't miss this chance!" Conchita said, and she pulled me in the direction of the restaurant, but I refused at first because I was afraid; what if the bear came out and attacked us, what if the cops found us peeking through the back door, but Conchita whispered, "Please, please!" imploringly, with her hands tied together like she was praying; I just hoped for the best and let myself be dragged along, and when we reached the door we put our backs against it and lowered ourselves slowly until our bottoms reached the ground; we waited there without making a sound until we heard it again, the noise grew real and clear, and when we heard it Conchita and I started giggling like little girls, giggling so hard we had to cover our mouths; the desire to kick the ground in excitement was so powerful I felt like I was gonna pee in my pants; "What do we do, what do we do?" I mouthed to Conchita, and she just made the sign of "Shhh!" with a finger on her lips, and then we heard the sound of claws thrashing through plastic, searching for food; I imagined the bear sitting on the floor, mountains of paper and plastic trash and a mess of metallic trays all around him; his furry brown chest sprinkled with bread crumbs and threads of transparent plastic dangling from his snout; "He smells funny," Conchita whispered after a while; "I know," I whispered back because he did; a spicy smell similar to wet lamb's fur reached my nose; from time to time the thrashing sound would stop and we'd hear brief grunts or movement around the door, and that was when I felt his heavy and lonely presence close to us; I felt him grand and alive and lost; "Your kids won't believe their ears when you tell them this, Susy girl," Conchita whispered in my ear; I looked at her, and she looked back; I wanted to tell her something, but I didn't; I just reached out for her hands and grabbed them; I closed my eyes and saw myself back in Cuévano, stepping down from the bus with my hands full of gifts for my little ones; I saw them waiting for me by the road again, my Pedro and my Santiago and my Adrián taller than the last time I saw them, much taller now but happy to see me come home at last; Conchita and I stayed like that until the thrashing sound resumed; "He's got to stop eating those muffins," she whispered in my ear, and I had to nod; "I just hope he knows where the bathrooms are already," I said and we couldn't contain a laugh; and then we felt it, his big nose sniffing at our butts under the door, the charged, wild stuffy air that came out of his nostrils warming the ground and tickling us through the polyester of our pants; then he leaned against the door and we felt a quick and strong push, and I froze; I felt goose bumps all over my arms; the laugh was gone; I eyed Conchita to check if she was scared, and she had this big, peaceful beam on her face; I made a sign to her that meant we needed to leave and she made a sign back that meant, "Not yet, let's stay a little longer, please!" but then we felt it, another push on the door, stronger and violent this time around; I shrieked, and Conchita shrieked too, nothing else needed to be said after that; we just jumped out of the ground and started running; we crossed the empty parking lot in seconds, I hadn't run so fast since I was a kid back in Cuévano, and as we ran we laughed; we laughed and laughed until we reached the bus stop, completely out of breath.

# BETTER LATITUDE

It didn't rain that Thursday afternoon, but the air tumbled over the city, old and musty, as if rolling out of a drawer that had been closed a long time. It was Laureano's last week of school. I picked him up late because I'd had to take care of a last-minute walk-in at the office, and treated him to McDonald's. You know your son; you know how much he loves that shit, and *I know, I know* it's bad for him, but I wished for us to be in a festive mood. I didn't want to go home right away. I needed my sore mind and his relentless energy to rest somewhere else.

I drove to the McDonald's on Barranca del Muerto, the huge one overlooking Periférico that has an enormous play-ground out front—I'm sure you don't know which one I'm talking about, for you'd never set foot in such a place anyway; you said that American fast food was tacky, that only wannabes and the poor craved it. Laureano didn't eat one single Chicken McNugget. He gulped down his fries and orange juice as fast as he could and darted to the playground, as if they were giving away lollipops there. He spent a lifetime in the ball pit, leaping and jumping and splashing furiously, surrounded by kids who looked younger than he was. They regarded him with caution and kept their distance, for he seemed too adamant about the whole business of having fun, as if it were a dead-serious matter. I remained at the table where we'd eaten, writing your name on the burger wrapper, an orphan french fry as a pen and ketchup as ink, watching Laureano through a large window below a sign that read

WELCOME TO PLAYPLACE

He looked like a frantic dolphin trying new tricks in the open sea, riding the waves of a multicolor storm. I tried to stay present, watch him go mad, but my mind was stuck with you.

Four weeks had passed since I'd last seen you, since the three of us had eaten dinner together. It was a Wednesday. You stayed over, we slept together but didn't make love—I had my period. The next morning you sat next to Laureano at the kitchen table and watched him scarf down a bowl of cornflakes with cold milk while you drank black coffee and complained that you felt exhausted. You said you were reaching that age when one always feels tired no matter how much one sleeps. I felt like I'd reached that age some time ago but didn't say anything. What was the point of discussing inevitable miseries with you so early in the morning, minutes from your departure? Laureano got ready for school and when you both were in the car I asked if we should wait for you that night. You asked what day it was. I said it. You considered it. You said you were not sure you'd be back in time for dinner, but that you'd come back for sure. I stayed at the curbside, watching your car until it turned the corner and I never saw it or you again. The morning lit with clouds, the shades of green in the tree leaves and the fuchsia blossoms of the bougainvillea creeping down the wall at the entrance of the house; all had grown pale as if it had trouble breathing, paler than every color in Mexico City has ever been since I can remember.

We left McDonald's in that deadly hour of the afternoon that's neither lunch nor dinner time and when people at restaurants seem out of place. We came home and I said, Laureano, it's bath time. He begged me to let him go outside and hang out in the tree house. I couldn't believe his stamina. I felt tired all the time, it overwhelmed me to see this kid boasting of his energy, to see him only wanting to have fun, as if nothing else mattered. I wanted him to take a bath as soon as possible, for he'd been playing in that filthy ball pit barefoot and he hadn't washed his hands since. I didn't even want to think about the germs that stuck to his feet, his face. I wasn't in the mood to argue, so I let him go.

An hour passed and he was still out there. It was that moment of evening right before darkness breaks. The sky drew white and I felt winter had reached us again even though it was late June. I slid the backdoor open and called for Laureano. He didn't reply. I called him again. Your son, stubborn as a stale loaf of bread. I started in his direction, but suddenly his freckled face stuck out of one of the little windows and he said he was coming. He had this big, insuperable grin on his face. This little you.

Laureano jumped down from the porch of the tree house and ran to me with his cheeks flushed and gleaming. I said that it was bath time. He stopped dead in the middle of the yard and said I wouldn't believe who he'd been hanging out with. I had zero interest in finding out. I'd been up since six thirty in the morning, it had been a hard day at the office, four pedicures (old diabetic widowers, customers delightful as hemorrhoids), one case of severe athlete's foot, and one surgery to fix a good pair of nasty ingrown toenails. I had no energy left for riddles, but Laureano insisted that I guess. I mentioned some of his stuffed animals by name—Denver, the giraffe; Pensa-cola, the rooster; Pompeya, the sheep—but it was no use. He giggled; he shook his head with tenacity and said I'd never find out. I give up, I said, and he revealed he'd been hanging out with you. Laureano's eyes shone disarmingly, enraptured by jubilance. Little bastard happy like it was Kings' Day. The flesh of my legs turned into Jell-O, squishy and tremulous. My lips quivered. For a second, I hated him. I wanted to slap him in the face and hug him and burst into tears and yell

WHY ARE YOU DOING THIS TO ME

all at once, but I didn't. I imagined your lanky, six-foot-tall frame curled up inside that toy house next to our son, your salt-and-pepper hair scratching against the ceiling like a por-cupine with a rash, your long, infinite arms and your strong hands struggling to fit in that box, and the image was heart-breaking and hysterical. I asked Laureano to tell me more, but he said there wasn't much else to it. I forced a smile and cleared my throat and repeated, *bath time*. I held his hand. It was warm, soft with the newness and the hope and the fear-lessness of youth. We came inside. I looked forward to a drink.

When Laureano was stripping off his clothes in the bath-room he said I had to wash his ears thoroughly because you'd taken a look at them and said they were yucky. I asked him to say that again, and he did. Did you really check his ears when you guys were together? Little you confirmed and added that you'd checked his fingernails and his toenails and his teeth as well. I grabbed him by the shoulders, bent down, and explored his ears. That's when he said you'd deemed his fingernails and toenails neat, but that he could do a better job brushing his teeth. That's when I thought

90

## YEAH, RIGHT

A month had passed since he'd last seen you too. He seemed to be missing you as much as I was, but we hadn't talked about it. I knew he'd long grown used to your intermittent presence in our lives. He already knew you'd only spend a couple nights a week at home, that you'd drop him off at school every now and then. I didn't think it was necessary to address your absence just yet.

Then one evening at dinnertime he asked when you were coming back. We were finishing dessert. While I searched for an answer to the very question that haunted me every day, I offered him more lemonade. He gave me those eyes of yours that meant, *cut the crap, Mom.* I said you'd had to make a long trip for your job, longer and farther than usual, which was why you hadn't been able to come home or even call, but that you would, soon. He asked where you'd gone. Little cactus thorns pierced my lungs. China, I said. He asked where in China. I wanted him to shut up and stop hurting me, but I said you hadn't gone to Shanghai or Beijing, but to a town in the south, a village so small its streets weren't paved but made out of powder, its airport so humble only one plane landed there every week. He looked at me with his eyes wide open in amazement, and I felt abominable for taking advantage of his six years of age. He wanted to know the name of the town. I said I couldn't remember, for I'd hardly heard of it myself, and coaxed him to finish his fruit salad. He begged me to look it up on the world map we'd given him for his birthday, the one we'd just stuck on the wall above his bed. It was past eight. It was time for bed; we'd do that in the morning, I promised him. Little fucking you insisted, insisted, insisted, his fruity-smelling voice growing louder and more unsettling, until I conceded. He charged out of the kitchen. I trailed behind him dragging my feet, wishing I could turn water into whiskey, wishing I'd made wiser decisions in my life.

I found Laureano standing barefoot on his bed, his index finger crawling along the mustard-colored corner of Asia, looking for you. No, it isn't Hong Kong; that is actually a pretty big city, I said. He asked if it was Beihai, or Shantou, or Simao, or Xiamen, his finger hopping across the far-off land. He called out the names he found in southern China, and he read them fast. He was full of wonder, so smart and small. I thought about all the disgraces life had in store for him and how handsome he was and how well he could read at such an early age, a jumble of thoughts that made me feel very lonely. I wanted to kiss him forever and run away with him to another planet where I hadn't met you and he was still my son, somewhere else where you were a different man and you were with us, but I just stood on the bed embracing him from behind, our feet touching on the duvet, my index finger pointing to the tiniest, most isolated spot I could find. All he said was

WOW

He said it was far and tiny indeed. I said, now it's time for bed.

He didn't mention you again until that Thursday. I had no idea where you were and every day I'd wonder why you didn't even call. When he said you'd checked his feet and hands and face to make sure I was taking good care of him while you were away, I dismissed his daydream, his hallucination as a coping of sorts. But later that night, when Laureano was asleep, I climbed into the tree house to see if you were still there, if I could see you too. I couldn't fit. I didn't remember how small it was. How did you manage? How did you sneak through the house without my noticing? Why were you visiting only him?

I knew that one day you'd be gone for good. I knew that in the end, I'd raise Laureano on my own. We were twenty-five years apart. I had no doubt one day I'd have to give Laureano the news of your final departure. I'd played the scene in my mind so many times. I'd even practiced, trying different faces before a mirror like in a crappy flick: devastated, mad, resigned. Always the same line:

LAUREANO, DADDY'S GONE TO HEAVEN

You insisted on having him baptized and sending him to a Catholic school, so I thought that if I said:

LAUREANO, DADDY HAS DIED

the first thing he'd ask would be whether you'd made it. I knew I'd hesitate, and that would mortify him. In my rehearsals, you were granted instant forgiveness, eternal salvation.

I liked to think that once you were gone, I wouldn't have the nerve to keep sugarcoating shit for him, like I still do. I'd see myself becoming the badass honest mom I've never been:

No, Laureano,

GOD DOESN'T EXIST

and neither do heaven nor hell. That's the bullshit Daddy wanted to believe in because it made things easier for him. And, no, Mommy and Daddy were never married.

That wedding picture on my bedside table is not authentic, it's

## THE FAKEST WEDDING PICTURE EVER

The first time you asked to see a picture of our nuptial ceremony, I rented the dress at a costume shop and Daddy dressed in a tuxedo that wasn't bought for the occasion or anything stupid like that, and we got that picture taken at a photo studio near his office at lunchtime. And when I saw myself in that dress I wished we'd actually married, and when the photographer prompted us to smile I had to fight back the tears and I thought

## WHAT THE FUCK AM I DOING

in this hideous dress? Why am I ruining my life like this? And Daddy was constantly away from home not because of his job, but because he had another family and he lived with them, even after his wife died. Yes. Daddy loved you, Laureano. I think he really did, but he didn't love you enough. He didn't love me enough either. He said he did, but he didn't. He loved us the same way people like him love pedigree dogs, expensive cars, time-shares in Acapulco.

## WE WERE HIS PETS

an extravagant hobby he could afford.

And yet, I loved him. I really fucking did. It wasn't a matter of being smart or idiotic or brave or weak or strong. I only hope this never happens to you, my son. That you know you're falling fully, immensely, grandiosely, irreparably for someone who's going to fuck your life wholly, and still you can't help yourself.

Laureano finished school the following week and I enrolled him in English summer camp, so that I could continue to work in the mornings. On Sunday evening I called my parents, for the first time in years, to see if things were different now. For some reason I thought that my father would be aware of your disappearance and that he might have changed his mind. Perhaps he'd want to meet his grandson. Perhaps he'd even ask me to let Laureano stay with them over the summer. When he heard my voice on the line, he asked

ARE YOU STILL FUCKING THAT MAN

I wanted to tell him that you'd been gone for over a month, that I didn't know if you'd dumped me or died or what, but I just said yes, I was still with you.

SO YOU'RE STILL A WHORE

he said, and hung up.

Every evening, after dinner, Laureano would ask to go to the tree house so that he could play with you. Upon his return, he'd brag about all the fun things you guys had done together. Once, he brought his stuffed animals with him, not only Denver and Pompeya and Pensacola, but also José Alfredo, the boar; Acambay, the T. rex; and Blue Demon, the chimp. He crammed them all into his Spider-Man backpack, as if he were leaving home, and I watched him cross the backyard and rush up the rubber ladder at full speed, the backpack bouncing sideways against his scapulae. You dashing out to you. When he returned he said you had played Chapultepec Zoo. You'd incarnated the zookeeper and he the vet, and together you had cured all the zoo animals of a rare ailment that impeded them from chewing leaves. Another evening, he packed in *The Cat in the Hat Comes Back* and *Little Red Riding Hood*. Later he told me that you'd read them aloud, giving each character a different voice, performing the stories as if you were onstage, as many times as he'd asked.

I'd stay in the living room, looking from the distance at the tree house, trying to get a peek of the activity inside, waiting to see your suntanned, slightly wrinkled face appear through any one of those tiny windows, but nothing ever moved in there. Once I tiptoed across the backyard and got as close to the tree as I could, trying to overhear your allegedly delightful dad-son quality time, but the tree house was quiet, as if it had been empty forever, and the silence was only broken every now and then by the chirping of a squab calling his mother or the howl of a police siren coming from the deep of the city, large and threatening and sorrowful.

The next evening, when he was packing his stuffed animals, getting ready for another fun day at the zoo with his daddy, I asked him when you'd returned from China. We were in his room. His backpack was on the bed beside him, and he was pushing Denver in by the hoofs to make him fit. He looked up at the map above his bed, then turned to me with confused eyes, as if considering the question for the first time. He said he didn't know, and kept stuffing animals into the bag. As he walked away I realized I'd learned to hurt him without leaving marks, next time I might as well whip him on the soles of his feet. That night, he didn't report back to me about your trip. I didn't press further, and neither one of us mentioned China again.

96

. . .

I tried calling your office. Your assistant sounded frazzled, like she'd been through a horrible accident that had left her teeth broken and she'd had to keep them in her mouth. She inquired who I was, what I wanted. She didn't talk any-more—she'd learned to bark. I said I was your chiropodist and was calling because you'd missed a couple of appointments and you had another one coming up next week. She didn't reply. Rainy season had blasted the city at last. I could hear the vehicles swooshing against the flooded street in front of my office. Your assistant said you would be out of town for a while but that you'd get my message. She said it in a way that made me want to hang up. But would you be back in time for your next appointment? It was Friday, and I said you were scheduled for Monday. She told me again to leave a message.

On Saturday morning, Laureano said he wanted to go to the pool. Let's get out of town for a change, I said. I wanted to rid my skin of this sensation of crumpled brown paper bag that was eating it. I wanted to let the foreign blue and cloud-less sky of the rest of the world rub our bones with its aliveness. Let's go south, let's go for some heat! We packed towels and swimsuits and beach toys, and headed to Cuernavaca. Laure-ano even brought his stuffed animals. He grew excited about the possibility of taking them on a safari adventure; he said you wouldn't believe it when he told you all about the trip. I suggested we stop for lunch at one of the famous quesadilla stands—of course, you've no idea what I'm talking about— along the road right where Insurgentes ends and the Federal Highway begins, where there are trees taller than buildings and some parts of nature haven't been taken over by angst yet. But the traffic knot on Periférico grew tighter as we drove farther south. When we reached our exit, we couldn't continue. It was blocked by police patrols and cranes from the city's disease control department. Men in white overalls and blue breathing masks stood atop the cranes, retrieving dozens of human limbs that hung from the trees by the side of Periférico, as if severed arms and legs from bodies no one would ever locate were the city's newest fruit. I'd never seen anything like it before, only read about it in the paper, watched it on TV, refusing to give full credit to such reports. I couldn't help wondering whether any of those extremities were yours and whether that was the reason you'd disappeared, but the thought was too painful to bear. I wondered whether the mothers of those who'd lost their appendages knew what had happened to their sons, and I felt sorry for them. Laureano asked what these white men in masks were doing. I said, nothing,

## COVER YOUR EYES

and I threw my copper cashmere cardigan over his head and ordered him to remain covered until I said otherwise. After a great while we reached the next exit. I took it and parked the car, my heart thumping like a boom box. I wondered why I'd told my father that I was still with you. I wondered why I was ever with you, and I felt you growing exotic inside of me. I wondered what Laureano had seen before I covered his eyes, and what kind of feelings, what concept of the world he'd nurture when he understood this moment. I remembered there was a Radisson on the other side of Periférico, and I told Laureano we couldn't go to Cuernavaca, but we'd still go to the pool. I stroked his legs and then his shoulders and his back, as if it were freezing outside. I pulled him close to me, straining my body across the gearshift to embrace him. He asked if he could uncover his head now. Little you's voice muffled and shivery. He said the cardigan was itchy and making him hot.

On Monday morning I called your office again. I explained once more about your appointments, and your assistant repeated what she had said on Friday, like an automatic voice-mail greeting. I said that on your last visit we'd taken some samples of your foot skin and I needed to discuss the results with you urgently. She ignored my absurd excuse and said: Dr. Guevara,

WOULD YOU LIKE TO LEAVE A MESSAGE FOR HIM

She sounded warm and sympathetic this time, as if she knew me well and worried for me, like my mother did when she still spoke to me. I tried to imagine her at her desk, answering my call, and I realized I knew very little about her. I knew she was old, like you. The only time you'd talked about her you said she'd been working for you since 1970. I said it was the year I was born. You thought about that for a moment, as if considering a certain logic between both facts, and you said you'd never replaced her with someone younger because you didn't want your wife to think you could cheat on her with your own assistant. Your wife was still alive; Laureano did not yet exist. I thought our thing was simply something crazy and adventurous, a fling without consequence. Still, it hurt me to hear you talking about your assistant like that. You didn't add that you'd kept her because she was good at her job or because she was loyal or because she knew you like she inhabited your brain. I realized you had a capacity for disposing of people like they were ziplock bags, but I considered this trait of yours the same way I did tragedy or bad luck, only affecting other people, never myself.

I was running out of options, so I asked to talk with your oldest son instead. She remained quiet on the line.

## WHO ARE YOU?

she asked, finally. Her voice soured, heavy and low, back in bitter bitch mode. I said I wanted to know what had happened to you. I said you hadn't come home in weeks. I said I had a six-year-old who was losing his mind because he was missing you terribly, and I needed to know what was going on. She went quiet and put me on hold, her silence replaced by a sugary and unnerving rendition of Ravel's *Boléro*. Several minutes passed. I heard my 10:00 a.m. appointment arrive in the waiting room — an old, chatty Spanish émigré named Silverio, Don Silverio, who'd tell me stories during therapy about his happy childhood in Teruel before the Civil War tore his family apart and he was sent to Mexico, along with other children, away from their families for what became forever. Your assistant came back on the line and asked for a different number where I could be reached. I gave her my cell phone and she said, no, she needed my home number. She sounded like a different person. Your assistant, or whoever was now on the line, said they would call me back in thirty minutes. I'd better be there, this better be real. When I hung up my legs were shaking. I started to feel sick, a hole growing in my stomach. I rushed to the bathroom to throw up but nothing came out; I saw my body jerking in front of the toilet, stooping in spasms. I saw it from outside, as if my body and my mind had split into two different entities.

I refreshed myself, went back to the office, grabbed my purse, and dashed away. On my way out I told Esmeralda, my assistant, to cancel my appointments for the day. Out of the corner of my eye, I saw Don Silverio rise from his chair, his big, plump, freckled, rosy hands gripping the handle of his walking cane, producing the bright, hopeful grin he always did when he saw me, but I didn't stop to salute him. I didn't know what I could possibly say.

Laureano was already playing in the ball pit when your other son arrived. I'd chosen a table right by the window, so that I could observe Laureano through the glass. Victoriano sat down across from me. He studied me in silence. He looked fascinated and disgusted by my looks and my age. I felt like a painting by Francis Bacon, repulsive and riveting. I admired the features of his sandpapered face, searching for traces of you. Physically he must have resembled his mother. He was handsome and dull in ways you aren't, but he was you nonetheless. You'd once mentioned he was older than I was, but he looked younger. His presence radiated singleness, childlessness, all the flaws that distinguished him and distressed you. But he'd inherited your immense cognac eyes, and the corners of your lips, turned up, as if pointing to the sky.

Victoriano looked out the window, searching for his half brother, and spotted him immediately. I could see it in the way his facial muscles tensed and his body shifted position. That moment you find yourself in someone else. The horrifying instant life reveals itself before your eyes.

He stared, in silence. Outside, in the ball pit, Laureano was a firework. Your son's gaze softened for a moment. He looked taken, looking at you.

He asked Laureano's age. I replied and he nodded, his eyes shut for a moment. Then a grin. The same grin you'd offer before uttering a cruelty. Before he could say anything, I asked whether he knew anything about Laureano or me. I knew he didn't. I just wanted to hurt him first, even though he had the upper hand.

He didn't answer. He asked

DOES HE CARRY OUR NAME

I hated you in that moment for making me go through this humiliation. And I hated myself for letting it happen.

YOU DON'T KNOW YOUR FATHER, DO YOU

I said. Victoriano looked away from Laureano, whose acrobatics he'd been chasing around the ball pit, and looked me in the eye. He said he couldn't care less about Laureano or me. He wasn't there because of us, but because of his family, yours. He needed to know if Laureano had your name, his name. I asked what difference that could possibly make. He said the steps he'd follow to take care of us depended on my answer. He didn't sound menacing or concerned, just arrogant. I asked what he was talking about. I said he didn't need to take care of us. I hadn't called your office looking for help. I just wanted to know where you were. He looked at me strangely. I felt his contempt. But there was something else. I said, please, I need to know

WHAT HAPPENED TO HIM

He crossed his arms, rested his elbows on the table, averted his gaze, and sighed. He stared back at me with the same strange expression, full of rage and sadness, and looked away, shaking his head. He whispered: *little motherfucker*, and chuckled sourly. He said *little motherfucker* almost paternally, almost stoically, as if he were acknowledging your motherfuckerness, or his, or Laureano's, or all of them, the inherent motherfuck-erness of all men, as if celebrating it and suffering it all the same. I struggled to remain in control, and not to let my eyes betray the terror I felt for me and for Laureano and for what-ever could happen next. Then he got serious, he looked at me again, and then he said it. He said you'd been kidnapped the last Thursday of May, on your way home from work. He said they knew very little else about your whereabouts, only that they had proof. I asked what kind of proof, but he refused to elaborate. He said it flatly, as if he were the mere herald of an official dispatch and not your son, but his eyes betrayed him. They brimmed with fear and despair. I realized you'd disap-peared from them the same day you'd disappeared from us, and that made me resent you less. I thought of you, alone and afraid, and for a moment I felt I'd do anything to help you, to keep you from suffering. I looked at our son, smaller and wilder than ever. I couldn't fight back the tears. I sobbed qui-etly, straining my neck to face the window, covering the side of my face with my hand so that your son wouldn't see me cry.

In the reflection of the window, everything inside McDon-ald's swelled, deformed and translucent, bright red, yellow, white. In a separate room, a birthday party was taking place. A woman from the staff walked into the room holding a pink Barbie-themed cake with a number 5 for a candle. The group burst out in screams of excitement when they saw it and started singing "Las Mañanitas" in unison; even the birthday girl did, but I didn't hear any of that. All I could hear was other kids yelling, the buzz of customers going through their meals and shuffling around, and rancid pop music from the eighties blasting from speakers, Chaka Khan and Sheena Easton and Julio Iglesias, one after the other, while my watery eyes sought refuge from your sons and from your fate, from the motherfuckerness of all of it, in that lucky girl's birthday party which I couldn't hear but I could see and I could feel. I envied that poor little girl and I envied her family and her friends, and in that moment I wished that the wishes she'd wish when she blew out her candle wouldn't come true.

Victoriano remained quiet while I pulled myself together. He looked out the window, mesmerized by the spectacle of his own kin taking dips and splashing waves in the rubber. He said that if Laureano only carried my name then we were in less danger. Otherwise, we needed to act fast. It was the only time he referred to us, not only Laureano and me but also them, your family, as a unit. I said of course he had your name and he said, then we needed to flee the country as soon as possible. I asked why and he said because our safety was in peril, not only mine and Laureano's, but theirs as well, your siblings' and their spouses' and your grandchildren's too, and I asked how come and he said because they couldn't afford for other members of the family to be kidnapped. I didn't know what else to say, so I didn't say anything. I felt dreamy, slow, chocolatey, strawberry-y, sundaey, french fry-y, birthday cakey. I'm sure he faked it, but he said,

I'M SORRY

but that he was serious. I said we couldn't leave, I had my own business, I had a mortgage, a car. I simply couldn't drop everything and run away. He gave me a condescending look and said,

SO YOU'RE A WORKING SINGLE MOM, HUH

He said it was moving. He said I sure was an inspiration to other women. He said now it was clear to him I was with you only because I loved you.

## OR WAS IT THE SEX

he asked, the motherfucker. I wondered how much you'd hate
me if you knew what I was going to do, and I realized I might
never see you again. I wished someone were next to me in
that moment, my parents, the friends who had stopped talking
to me, to stand up for me. I felt like rising from that uncomfortable plastic seat attached to the table, where my butt had
grown cold and numb, fetching my son and walking away, but
I decided I didn't want to.

## YOUR FATHER WAS RIGHT, YOU'RE SUCH A PUSSY

I said, and stood up slowly, hoping that it would make me look
taller than I am. I grabbed my purse. I took the red plastic
tray with the burger I didn't finish and chicken nuggets Laureano didn't eat and the cups of soda, and tossed everything
into the trash. I was so nervous I even discarded the tray. I felt
your son's heavy gaze follow me. I feared he'd come after me,
but he didn't. I did my best to ignore him, knowing I couldn't
afford it but doing so anyway, and I never once turned back. I
just walked away into the PlayPlace.

Some kids stopped playing and gawked at me, frozen, as if I
were Gulliver's girlfriend, taking over their realm. Laureano kept
swimming and splashing in the ball pit, oblivious of my presence. I removed my earrings and put them in my purse, left the
purse on the floor, took off my shoes, and inched into the pool.

Laureano cheered when he saw me and asked what I was
doing there, surprised, as if he were on the concerned kids' side.
He stood waist deep in the sea of rubber balls. I hugged him as
best as I could, feeling his body frail and warm against mine, his

soft hair that smelled like home, never wanting to let him go. In his ear I said that every time we came I'd see him having such a wonderful time in that pit and I'd always wanted to join in the fun, but I'd never been brave enough to do it. He said that was pretty cool, and took a dive; his head disappeared amid waves of plastic balls, red and purple and green and yellow and blue. I'd always been worried those balls were too rough or cold to the touch or too smelly, let alone all the germs they surely carried, but they weren't. They felt soft and balmy. They smelled like lemon trees. I looked back at the restaurant, searching for Victoriano, but he was gone. I lay faceup on the surface of that sea, and let it carry my weight. I felt time pass and the scream of kids grow thin around me, until a young man from the staff tapped me on the shoulder and very kindly, while I opened my eyes, said that the day had turned into night and that it was probably a good idea for me and my kid to go home.

When we got to our house, Laureano asked me to let him go out to you. I had very little to say, so I said okay, and he dashed to his room. Minutes later he returned with the backpack on his shoulders.

On his way out, I asked if he'd give you a message. He said of course he would, and his freckled face blushed as if he wondered whether he'd learn something about you, or me, or both, that he shouldn't, something he'd long wished he would. He was so beautiful and faint in the yellow night light. I said

TELL DADDY I MISS HIM

His face grew serious and sagged, he looked like the man he would become one day, the man who would forget how to splash

106

into pits of colorful infiniteness and be merry, the man who one day would hurt and be hurt by the world of men and everything that came with it. He approached me slowly and gave me a hug that encompassed all his little, helpless might. He buried his bony, perfect cheek and your scratchy, everlasting hair in my tummy, and he promised he'd deliver my message to you.

I sat on the ottoman in the living room and watched our son cross the backyard in the charged, nocturnal air of the city that wanted to push us out. I saw him walk on the dewy grass wearily, as though the animals he was carrying were real, living things, and it seemed to me that the distance that separated our home from the tree house had grown fathomless. It was a velvety, navy, screamless night that felt stolen from a better latitude of the earth.

# HER ODOR FIRST

I enter my baby's room and find him against the bed, knees nailed to the carpet, branchy hands clasping the comforter like running sand. He doesn't notice me. My baby sees me, hears me, no more. I carry on to his dressing room and busy myself caressing his button-down shirts, smoothing out his polos and jerseys, which still smell like Suavitel, ancient and upsetting, like the back of the house always did when I was alive. My specter cuddles in sleeves and collars and cuffs crisp and free of wrinkles, as if their fabric were made of clouds, all of his clothes pure white, because ever since my baby became a man that's the only color he's worn on top. My baby, the once mighty and immaculate. He was an angel that used to thunder through the days, thrashing others like they were flies, before this afterlife.

I call him my baby but he doesn't know. He never knew. My baby, bold and ill-tempered and cute as hell since the day he was born. He still possesses formidable arms like razor blades and bright, sunflower hair, like his mother's. She took pride in giving birth to him, to all of them, but my baby was mine all along. His demeanor used to make me shiver, not only me but everybody else in the house, siblings and servants alike. Now his hands tremble and his eyes tumble darkened with the trueness of fear, with the absoluteness of death that I and everybody else in the back of the house had long experienced like the inevitable everyday occurrence that it is, that simply happens to you when you're an ordinary nobody, but he, they, hadn't, safe in this fortressed realm, until now. None of them had yet been touched by the one mighty will that makes us all equal. The poor, stupid kids. My baby and his siblings, now gone away.

They now know loss, and from this distance, I smile.

My baby took refuge in his room as boxes kept arriving at the door. Boxes brimming with so-called precious things that the siblings left behind. It was distressing and exhilarating all at once watching them scramble. They grew so scared after receiving Don Victoriano back in parts that they ran away, as quickly as they could, shitting in their fancy pants and pencil skirts, babies again, dragging stinking diapers around the house until I changed them, sometimes immediately, if their mother or Don Victoriano were around, but frequently only after they had rashes around genitals and cracks, for I needed these kids that would cry for everything to learn something real about pain. Alas, just a bit.

Expensive paintings that looked as if they had been drawn by fools, silver tea and cutlery sets inherited from their parents and grandparents, leather-bound photo albums filled with thousands of family pictures, extensive records of their decades of glory—the happy, selfish, arrogant days that preceded this dismay. Pictures where I appear every now and then, sneaking into focus at birthday parties while helping their mother serve the cake.

My baby had those countless boxes stored inside the house,

in the hallways and the mezzanines, the living room, the dining room, the library, the playroom, Don Victoriano's, his siblings'. Every room but his own. Only my baby remains in the house and yet a flock of boxes without tags, labels, or names has been shoveled in to keep him company, to shield him. The boxes multiplied like a plague. In a matter of days they were everywhere, like larvae in a bad dream.

Stacks, rows, piles, heaps and mounds of boxes lay heavy along the hardwood, the marbled floors. They've formed narrow labyrinthine passageways that connect one room with the next. It's become impossible to take in the full size of the spaces, the beauty of their arrangements—this house was stunning and magnificent; their mother, I admit, had class—and the smells of Don Victoriano and the faint manly aroma of wood and tangerine that trailed after my baby when he still wore eau de toilette.

Their mother used to smell like a porcelain doll, flawless and inanimate, but her fragrance faded away shortly after she died. I made sure there were cut-glass vases with roses from the garden in every room for my baby and his siblings, Don Victoriano too, to forget her spell quickly—her odor first.

Now all you see is the maze of boxes, the corners of boxes, the crumpled fortress of boxes, and all you smell is the smell. The whole house reeks of rotten bark, the prickly way damp cardboard does. I drag myself along these box-carved narrow corridors, from kitchen to dining room, from the library to the billiard room, and the house tells me it's devouring itself.

I can hear it yell.

The father's house eating the children's.

Soon there won't be any trace of their existence. All of them gone. Only my baby, who always lived here, and the house stand. Still for me to care for. And me, in this disgrace.

Help me, God.

When my baby could still hear me I suggested that we store the boxes in the garage and the basement. There's enough room in the service areas of the house to put away the kids' leftovers, to secure the past behind walls, but he cried no. The eyes of my baby eloquent with fright, like a lightbulb about to burst.

My baby senses me as I'm coming out of the closet and he looks around, chasing my presence. He knows I'm here, we remain connected. But I can't meet his cornered-bull eyes. I can't touch his sagging face. From this distance, forced upon us by my fate, I can't soothe him. I can't caress his reddened cheeks and bring relief to his expression, wet, drunk, full of angst. I've never seen my baby like this before, and for once I'm glad he can't see me either.

It's late October. The night air is sweet and cool. Life around the house has grown stale; it's been several weeks since the children fled. Nothing moves. If you stand still and listen carefully, you can hear echoes of the lives that this house held, the children's, the parents', ours, fading out.

"How come boxes keep arriving?" at some point my baby asked. It was late September, days before I tripped on the corner of a box as I was coming out of the kitchen and fell, my forehead hard and irremediable against the corner of a mahogany chest, on my way to the dining room, where my baby still had dinner at regular hours. I was still providing him with a regular service, trying to maintain a regular life. Alas. "When is this going to end?" I didn't know what to say.

"Dinner is ready, Vic. Are you coming down?" I wish I could say to him right now. On a night like this I'm sure he'd order something warm, nice and cozy. Caldo tlalpeño or cream of leek and potato soup. Handmade corn tortillas. A glass of red wine. Then he'd ask, "What's for dessert, Erme?" My baby, my sweet-tooth boy forever. I'd announce I made arroz con leche the way he liked it, al dente, very creamy, with an extra pinch of cinnamon. And he'd beam, full of bliss. My baby backing down for once, revealing his harmless side, only to me. Because it was only to me he never expressed contempt. I was the only one who never feared him. I was the only one he really ever loved.

I'm sure I was the reason he never left.

Now I'm standing right before him, by his filthy, messed-up bed, hearing his derailed breathing, about to choke, watching the collapse of his family through his own.

He can't see my tears. My serenity escapes him.

# BAREFOOT DOGS

It's not the baby, or the dog, or the memories, or the ghosts that wakes me up. It's the delivery trucks. I hear the whoosh of their sliding metal doors, the clanking when the drivers slam them shut, the thuds against the asphalt as the drivers unload beer kegs and crates full of produce and groceries. I hear the rusty doors of the businesses down the street as they open for the day—the supermarket on the ground floor of our building, the pharmacy with its green flickering neon cross at the corner, the bar to our left. To our right. There's a bar every hundred feet in Madrid. They reek of smoke, chorizo, and sweat. Madrid is a bar that never shuts. Noisy and full of boisterous people who always seem unnervingly happy.

The sounds of the city blast into our room as soon as dawn breaks. The room where Catalina, the baby, and I sleep overlooks the street, and we keep the windows open to let a breeze in. There are no curtains or blinds on the windows because we don't care about privacy and security here. We don't have to worry about that anymore.

Six a.m. in Madrid and I'm already awake. And hot. The T-shirt I wore to sleep is damp and sticky. It's white, but my perspiration has left peach-colored stains on the chest. September like I've never experienced it before. Oppressive and devoid of rain.

Six a.m. in Madrid means 11:00 p.m. in Mexico City. Back home it's yesterday. Still night. Streets packed with people getting ready to celebrate Independence Day. Streets where I grew up, became a father, and lost mine. Masaryk, Reforma, Periférico Norte, Montes Elíseos. Full of cars. Headlights on.

I miss the nights.

I rise from bed and peek at the crib. The baby's alive. He's moving. Already awake. The jet lag hit him hard, and two weeks after landing in Madrid, he still wakes up too early. Outstretched arms and legs. Drooling.

He makes gurgling noises that Catalina insists are the beginnings of words—she thinks he is precocious. I don't know much about babies myself—I was the youngest at home—but those noises sound more like he's drowning in his own saliva.

I approach the crib, and the stench of shit and scented diaper hits me in the face. I take the baby out and feel him looking at me. I avoid his eyes. He is an exact replica of me. It gives me the creeps.

I place him on the bed and start to change his diaper. It's overloaded. His sky-blue onesie is a mess. I clean him up as best as I can, but the whole room now reeks of shit.

I wish it smelled like baby wipes, flowery and powdery, the way I think babies should smell when I look at the picture of the gorgeous, merry baby printed on the container of baby wipes.

The baby was born a few days after the first box arrived. Twenty-three hours into labor, he got stuck. Dr. Castañeda had to perform a C-section and wrestle him out. He handed him to me, and I had to cut the umbilical cord. I couldn't help thinking about my father, the suffering he was experiencing. I didn't have the guts to refuse, but I closed my eyes when I severed the cord. It didn't feel human; it felt like cutting a copper wire in two. When I first looked at his face, he was covered with blood and goo. Purple and swollen, but already a mirror. He opened his eyes and rolled them around the room until he rested them on me. We looked at each other for a spell before I passed him to Catalina. It was the last time I looked. The next day, when Dr. Castañeda stopped by to check on Catalina and the baby, he confessed it had been one of the hardest deliveries of his career. He sounded apologetic and embarrassed. Catalina and I were speechless. My fingertips tingled with panic. I realized that at some point my son would die, and that there wouldn't be anything I could do about it. I feared him for the first time, as I feared that anything could happen to him. That afternoon, I asked the hospital to assign a bodyguard to us and the baby.

I get him in a fresh, clean onesie, and place him alongside Catalina. She's still sleeping. She sleeps a lot these days. She says she hasn't recovered yet. She says she feels as sleepy as she did during the first trimester of pregnancy, but she didn't sleep that much back then.

I rub her shoulder gently and whisper her name.

"What is it?" she says, her eyes still closed. Her voice is heavy.

"It's Belisario," I say quietly. "I think he's hungry."

Catalina pulls up her T-shirt and bares a breast full of milk. She brings the baby's mouth close to her and plugs him in. Belisario starts to suck like an animal; the sounds he produces are primitive and primal. And squeaky. As if his lips or Catalina's nipple, or both, were made out of rubber.

Whenever he eats, I take the chance to peek at his face. He's tightly attached to Catalina's breast, and this pressure deforms the shape of his nose, redefining his features. His cheeks are endless and rotund. His lips are redder. His frown furrier. He doesn't look like my son. He's a watchable, bearable stranger.

Catalina remains asleep. She manages to feed him while she dreams. I envy her. The baby's presence, his mere touch, seems to make her happy even when she's not awake.

Twenty minutes later the squeaking stops, and the baby starts to moan. He wants the other breast. Whenever he's tired, or hungry, or if he needs a clean diaper, he grumbles. He hardly cries.

In one clumsy, acrobatic movement, Catalina scoops him up and switches position. The baby's now on the other side of the bed and hooked up to the other breast. She's a bear with her cub.

The squeaking resumes. The walls in the room are naked, like the rest of the apartment. We wanted to bring our furniture from Mexico City with us, but we didn't have time. We wanted to find a new home for our palm plants, but we couldn't. The day we left, Catalina and I dragged them out to the backyard, hoping that they would catch the summer rain and make it. On our first days in Madrid, when we started looking for a place to live, we were offered furnished flats in fancier districts, but we turned them all down. The idea of using someone else's furniture was humiliating and depressing. We settled for this empty apartment on Guzmán el Bueno Street in the Argüelles neighborhood, on the second floor of a gray building from the mid-Franco era.

Someone at the Mexican embassy suggested Ikea. On our first visit we bought the bed, the crib, some chairs, a table, a couch, cutlery, blankets. It was fun and cozy. It seemed like a newfound home, orderly and safe. Everything was so inexpensive we could have afforded half the store, so on our second trip we went crazy buying candle holders, framed photographs of skylines, pillows, cactuses, handwoven baskets, stuffed snakes. In our apartment, the things that we bought felt cheap and used, like hand-me-downs. We went back the next day and returned almost everything. We have a TV that we got at El Corte Inglés. When the baby's asleep and we want to stop talking about Mexico or thinking about my father, we turn it on. We laugh at the way people speak here on TV; everybody sounds pompous or impertinent. Late-night shows feature people who get naked in front of the cameras or insult each other with phrases like *Me cago en tus muertos* or *Hostia puta*, that no one would dare utter back home. We watch TV a lot, but we don't watch news.

Belisario finishes breakfast. Catalina's nipple hangs in the air, glossy purple and blistered, until she pulls down the T-shirt and cuddles back in bed. I place the baby back in the crib. His eyes chase mine, but I look at his knees, his toes. I turn on the mobile that hovers above his head, and a herd of stuffed horses chase each other in circles.

I need coffee. I head for the kitchen.

In the living room I find Zurbarán stooped over a pool of something visceral, throwing up. His belly lets air in and out heavily, like a squeaky toy. The puddle is almost his size, green and revolting; little dark red lumps float on the surface like islands of blood adrift in a sea of bile.

He notices me and squints; his little nugget starts to rattle. It's around the time I normally take him out for the first walk. We stroll around the neighborhood at least three times a day, but some days even four, five, especially if Catalina tries to get me alone with the baby. Zurbarán is my out.

He's a mutt, but he doesn't look like it, except for the tail and the crooked ears. When he was a puppy, the kids in the gated community back home used to mistake him for a German shepherd—it was hilarious to see their scandalized faces when I explained that he wasn't pedigree, that he was just a stray dog from the streets.

Catalina found him one evening when she was coming home from work, on the corner of Reforma and Prado Sur. He was just a pup, full of worms, his body the size of a human heart. Someone had macheted off his tail, but the abuser saved one caudal bone, a bright white tip collared by a rim of ruby flesh that eventually grew skin and hair, and that he now shakes like a single maraca whenever he's anxious or merry. But mostly anxious.

He throws up again. There's more blood. Last night he was fine. When we got his passport and immunization records back in Mexico, the vet said he looked healthy as a gem. He barfs silently. I don't know if it's the stench of baby shit or what, but the vomit doesn't have a particularly unpleasant smell. His front legs tremble each time he lurches forward.

I don't want this to be real. I need to wake up. I walk to the kitchen.

The size of the apartment isn't bad, but the kitchen, fuck. Our walk-in closet back home was larger than this. In Mexico, houses have separate laundry rooms. Washing machines would never be installed in the kitchen. The real estate agent said it was a regular kitchen by middle-class European standards. She said it as if it were a highlight.

Yesterday's coffee is in the carafe. I pour a cup and heat it in the microwave. It tastes trashy and metallic.

In Mexico, we'd never have to brew coffee ourselves.

I pour a second cup and go back to the living room, waiting to see Zurbarán ready for a walk, jumping high in the air like every morning. The puddle gone.

I reach the living room. The mess is still there. Zurbarán's lying next to it, belly and hind legs and paws soaked in vomit, eyes closed. I squat down next to him, and he opens his eyes. I breathe in, and the only smell that reaches me is the aroma of microwaved coffee.

In our room Catalina and the baby are now awake, lying in bed. The air is stifling. Down on the street, motorcycles dash by one after another, and two women are fighting over someone whose attention they're both after. The argument is getting heated, but neither Catalina nor the baby seems to care. He's playing with the tips of her frizzy brown hair. She's humming a tune I don't recognize. "Hey there," she says sweetly, giving me a lazy smile. "Come on, join us."

"Something's wrong with Zurbarán," I say. "Looks like he's been puking all night."

"What?" she asks, stroking the baby's back. The smile vanishes.

"There's a pool of vomit in the living room. There's blood in it."

"Oh my God." She covers her mouth. "Is he gonna die?"

"Don't know. I know nothing about sick dogs."

"What are we gonna do if he dies?" she whispers, as if she didn't want the baby to hear. Her face turns white, like the blanket.

"I don't know." My eyes fill with tears. Catalina, and the baby, and the room grow blurry in front of me.

The first box arrived six weeks after my father disappeared. We hadn't had any news of him yet. The kidnapping expert recommended that we all move to my father's house. One Saturday in early July, around noon, the doorbell rang. Ermelinda, one of the maids, answered the door. She came back to the living room saying a FedEx guy was asking for my brother.

Victoriano went outside and came back with a box. It wasn't a FedEx box; it was a regular box, one you could get for free at a grocery store, badly sealed. He said it was heavy and cold. The living room grew silent. Victoriano placed it on the table, and we all circled around it. The label said it had been sent by Alice, no last name. Everybody in the house sensed it had something to do with my father, so the maids and the gardener came out of the kitchen and joined us in the living room, but my brother asked them to leave. The label showed the box had been shipped from Wonderland, Texas. The kidnapping expert, Ramiro Alcázar was his name, opened his laptop and googled it, but he couldn't find the place. Catalina felt dizzy. I asked if she was okay. She said she was, but her face had turned pale. My sisters coaxed her to go upstairs. She was due in a matter of days. The women in our families would look at her swollen belly and say it was pointy. They'd say we were expecting a boy for sure. We had decided not to find out. I wanted it to be a girl, but I never told anyone. I couldn't bear the idea of having a boy.

The label read: "This is the first gift." Alcázar lifted the box, sensing its weight. He suggested it would be better if he opened it alone, but Victoriano and I refused to leave. He said we needed to be ready for whatever might be in that box, but my brother cut him off and yelled, "Open the fucking box already!" Alcázar slit the box top open with a cutter and took out a ziplock bag filled with ice. He slid open the bag and found another ziplock bag inside. He slid open the second bag and found my father's right foot.


It's around ten, and we're on our way to the vet. Zurbarán hasn't thrown up again since we left the apartment. He walks more slowly than usual and limps every now and then, but he seems as happy to be out in the sun as ever. I don't know how he pulls it off, this enthusiasm, blinding and absurd.

Buildings around us grow taller as we walk. Madrid is a maze of bricks and aluminum, dull facades, and dry, suffocating air. A desert of urban debris. Three a.m. back home. The city is more alive when it's dark than when the sunlight struggles to push through smog. Dew and quiet are blanketing Mexico City, and I'm here, at the other end of the planet. Stoplights blinking out of order, decorations of the Mexican coat of arms glowing on every corner, incandescent and meaningless. And someone's probably being pulped to death somewhere in the rough edges of the city, in the core of the city. The city, somewhere. Brutal and impossible to let go of.

The vet is located on Vallehermoso, a few blocks away from the apartment. Zurbarán and I pass in front of it from time to time, whenever I decide to walk him east instead of south. It's called Anubis Clínica Veterinaria, bookended between a futon boutique called Cha Chi Nap and Tintorería La Rosa de los Prodigios, a dry cleaner's.

Catalina is pushing the stroller forward with the baby inside. He's chewing on the sombrero of the stuffed Emiliano Zapata that my older sister Laura gave him as a farewell gift. She didn't lose her sense of humor after my father disappeared. She said Madrileños would look at Belisario with that toy and think we were a family of Zapatistas, exiles of a different kind. No one laughed.

I glance at the baby. He is determined to tear the outrageous toy apart. I suddenly wish I had the courage to hold him. Sing him to sleep. Comfort him in my arms. Make him feel safe.

We're about to enter the clinic when Catalina stops and says we need to talk first.

"Are the three of us going in there with him?" she asks.

I frown. I don't get where she's going.

"I don't think a veterinary clinic is the healthiest place for a young baby."

"Well," I say, peeking through the window, "looks like a pretty hygienic place to me. This is Europe. I bet those European cats and dogs are healthier than the three of us put together."

"Remember that nice playground I took Belisario to a couple days ago?" she asks. "It's just around the corner. Why don't you and him wait for me and Zurby there?"

I hate when she calls him Zurby. This is a mutt with a severed tail, not a goddamn poodle.

"Don't know. I think it's better if I take care of the dog. What if Belisario gets hungry and you're not there?"

"He just ate before we came," she says. "He'll be fine. I can take care of Zurby. You always take him out for walks. Let me give you a hand with him for once." And she adds, "Also, it would be great if you guys could spend some time on your own, mommy-free."

I glare at her.

"Why are you doing this?"

"What do you mean?"

"You know what I mean."

"I do?"

"Yes, you do."

She sighs and scratches the tip of her nose. The baby keeps gurgling; he's now shaking Zapata like he wants to break it.

"Let's not talk about this here, okay?"

"You brought it up, not me."

"I brought what up?"

"You know what. Don't pretend you don't know."

We look at each other. I fear I might have a panic attack right here. My eyes get moist. Hers too.


After the second box arrived, Alcázar advised us to move abroad; he said no one in Mexico could guarantee our safety anymore. Victoriano ordered everybody in the family to leave as soon as possible. We moved to Madrid because Catalina and the baby could get Spanish passports quickly. During the Civil War, her grandparents fled Toledo and ended up in Mexico City. When Franco died and the dictatorship ended, it was too late to go back.

When we landed in Barajas, no one was waiting for us.

Laura and her family moved to Austin; Carolina and her family to Palo Alto; Daniela and hers to Stamford. Victoriano is the only one who remains in Mexico, taking care of everything we left behind until he can leave too.

We don't know anybody here.

"You know I love you," Catalina mumbles. Her face is red, eyes swollen. The dog's taking a nap by the stroller's wheels. Beads of sweat break out on my sides, my chest, my temples. "But you can't keep doing this," she adds. "You have to be with him. He needs you."

It's getting hotter by the minute. The air is sandy and narcotic, and the sidewalk feels chewy under my feet. The honey-eyed scent of the sycamore trees that green Madrid's arid streets, and which I've never smelled before, gets stuffy in my nose.

"I take care of Zurbarán," is all I say. She doesn't challenge me. She looks at Belisario, who has thrust the toy aside and is now exploring his fingers with his mouth. I look at the dog, his ruby tongue dangling from his mouth.

"We'll be at the playground," she says quietly. "Meet us there when you finish."

I want to tell her I love her. Tell her I'm sorry we're going through this shit because of my family. Grab her and Belisario and Zurbarán, and take a cab to Barajas and get us flight tickets back to Mexico City and fuck the rest, but I just nod.

I pull Zurbarán gently by the leash, and the two of us walk into the vet.

The smell.

It reeks of dog food and birdseed and disinfectant. The AC must be broken; it's almost as hot in here as it is out in the street. High-pitched barks and running water and the muffled chatter of female voices come from the back of the clinic. The ceiling is too low; the neon lights, bright blue and sickening.

A young nurse with piercings and bright green hair checks us in. She's tiny like a hummingbird. It's hard to believe she could save any living thing's life, but she moves resolutely around the dog. She squats down next to him and pets him.

"You're such a handsome guy," she says. Zurbarán wags his whole body. Whenever he gets excited, he looks like he's dancing salsa. The nurse cracks up and pets him again, playing with his crooked ears. "What's wrong with his paws?" she asks.

"Oh, nothing," I say, surprised by the question. "I brought him in because he's been throwing up all night."

"I see," she says, the cheerful tone slipping. "But there's also something wrong with his paws, isn't there?"

"What do you mean?"

She holds one of the dog's front paws and carefully folds it up so I can see. Zurbarán lets out a short cry. The nurse stares at me. No longer charming or sweet. I avert my gaze to the tiled white, stained floor, and blink. Blink.

"See this paw?" she asks with severity. "Don't tell me you hadn't noticed."

The paw's pad is blistered and bleeding, a yellowish fluid mixed with blood. She comforts Zurbarán with little coos while she checks the other pads. All of them look the same. I don't know what to say. She rises and takes Zurbarán's leash away from me.

"What's his name?" she asks. I say it. She doesn't react. Doesn't say, "What an original name" or, "Cool!" the things I used to get when I introduced him to people back home. She tells me to take a seat, and coaxes Zurbarán to come along with her.

I watch the nurse and my dog walk away through a corridor decorated with posters of animals and one that shows Victoria Abril as she dressed in the movie *Kika*, petting a macaw, along with the caption "Tropical Birds Belong in the Wild!"

I'm alone in the waiting area. The silence swells achy in my ears.

We were not with my family when the second box arrived. After the baby was born, Alcázar suggested that we go to the family's weekend house in San Miguel de Allende. We'd feel more relaxed there, he said. Victoriano called one evening a few weeks later. Eva, our maid, picked up the phone and said we were busy giving Belisario a bath. Catalina was. I was in the bedroom, installing a play yard we'd received as a gift days before. While I inspected the instructions, I heard my wife in the bathroom say, "Who's my little marmot?" The smell of baby shampoo reached my nose, and I imagined Belisario covered in bubbles. I imagined us far away, in a place where the baby had just been born and nothing else had changed. I could almost bring myself to join Catalina in the bathroom to bathe our son together. It was a balmy moment of light, a lapse of happiness.

Eva knocked on the door. I said we were busy, and she replied that it was my brother. That it was an emergency.

"This is it, Martín," Victoriano said.

"What happened?"

"You guys need to come back right now. I think this is fucking it."

"Calm down." I heard my own voice shudder. "Tell me what happened."

He breathed heavily into the phone, as if he hadn't heard my question. I'd never heard Victoriano in such a state. He's the oldest son. Dad's golden boy. Everything Victoriano did was always so fucking wondrous in his eyes. Always so impossible to beat. But that evening he'd become frail and antsy, a damselfly.

He couldn't go on at first. He broke down on the phone. My heart started to pound. I was filled with anticipation and horror.

"Another box arrived," he mumbled after a while.

"What was in it?" I asked, my mind going blank, limbs numb.

"I can't say it on the phone. Come back as soon as possible; we'll talk here."

"Tell me what was in that box," I insisted.

In the bathroom, Catalina praised the little marmot for being such a sport. It was raining outside. I wondered if it was raining in Mexico City as well. I wondered about the size of this new box.

"Was it an ear?" I heard myself asking out loud.

Victoriano kept weeping, unable to reply. Something had changed between us. I felt so calm I was startled. Drunk with a feeling that was new to me.

"Tell me what was in the box."

"Are you gonna tell Catalina?" he finally said.

"What the hell do you care if I do? Was it a hand, his head?"

"Shut the fuck up. Please," he begged.

Once when we were young, I went into Victoriano's room and found him with a friend from school, jerking off together. I didn't understand what they were doing, but their alarmed expressions signaled that it was something of consequence. I closed the door and ran to the backyard, where I hid till the maid called us in for dinner. That night Victoriano came into my room. He approached my bed and promised that if I ever told anyone what I'd seen, he'd kill me with his own hands. I was four or five; he was already a teenager.

"What was in the box?"

In the bathroom, I could hear Catalina take Belisario out of the tub. "Oh, my! My little marmot has turned into a bunny!" she cheered. I imagined him smiling at her.

"It was the other foot, wasn't it?"

Victoriano didn't reply; he kept sobbing like the frightened little kid he never was. Seconds passed. I tried to picture my father, and I couldn't. I tried to picture Victoriano on the other end. The image made me feel far away from him.

"I'm sorry," I said at last. My voice was now as shaken as his. There we were, two little sissies on each end of the line. My father would have been ashamed.

"I'm so afraid," he mumbled. "I don't know what to do."

I wanted to tell him I knew exactly how he felt, but I didn't.

. . .

Hours later, a young doctor with a powerful mustache and a sorrowful gaze asks me if I'm the owner of the Mexican dog. I say I am. He introduces himself as Dr. Ybarra. He asks me to come with him to his office. He says we need to talk.

It's past two. Dawn is breaking back where I belong. Night has turned into ashes scattered across the firmament, turned into daylight. The city's waking up, still dead.

On our walk back from the vet, stores and offices close their doors as we pass, in preparation for lunchtime. Only bars and restaurants remain open. Madrileños flock to them en masse as if they were serving salvation.

Sun high in the sky, white and unforgiving. All around the world people are dying by the thousands. I am still alive. Why.

Zurbarán's paws are wrapped in bandages, his feet look like a ballerina's, but he doesn't limp anymore. He's a wonder of nature, a hallucination, a specter. We all are to some extent. Only we haven't noticed. We haven't decomposed yet.

I haven't told Catalina what the vet said; Zurbarán doesn't look that ill anymore. When we met them at the playground, she didn't ask questions. As if I'd simply come back from walking Zurbarán around the block. On our way home, she points out things that surprise her in the street, the word *béigol* on a sign, a white, silky skirt in a store display, the absence of electric cables hanging from poles. She's either fooling me, saving her resentment for when we get to the apartment, or letting go.

"Look at you, Mr. Pickle!" the doorman says when he greets us at the entrance to our building and sees Belisario in the stroller, napping. "Enjoying yourself in dreams!"

His name's Antonio, and he lives with his family on the top floor of the building. He stammers every now and then, and because he's from the south, he speaks very fast. Sometimes I catch only half of what he says. He's in his fifties, and his facial skin looks sunburnt after spending a monthlong vacation at the beach.

Mr. Pickle is a stupid name for a baby, but I don't complain.

"I had three boys, and they all look like their mother!" He bursts out in laughter. "But look at him, he's a little you, huh?" I forge a grin and look at Belisario. I rest my eyes on his dangling, blushed, sweaty earlobes. That's where I look in public, so people don't think I'm avoiding him.

"He is, right?" I chuckle, hands in my pockets. It sounds fake, but he doesn't know me that well. Catalina does, and I feel her stare, judging me.

Antonio notices Zurbarán's bandages. He asks what's happened. His inquisitiveness makes me feel nostalgic for the help we had back home. An ambulance rushes by. Madrid won't shut up.

"Oh, well," I say dismissively, "apparently he's having a bit of a hard time getting used to the Spanish heat. His paws are a bit sore, that's all."

Zurbarán is resting by the door, in the shade. He hasn't once tried to wiggle out of the bandages. Antonio pets him, playing with his ears. If I were the dog, I'd be sick of so much cooing, but he seems to like it.

"It's always hard to get used to a new place," Antonio says, and places his hand on my shoulder and squeezes gently. "I know what you guys are going through. I once was an immigrant myself. Have I told you the story of my family?"

He has, the very first time we met, when he noted our accents were different and asked where we'd come from, but he tells it again anyway.

"I was eight when we left Málaga; Dad couldn't make a living. We wound up in Paris; my parents landed jobs taking care of an apartment building on the Île de Saint-Louis. Dad,

Mom, Carmen, my sister, Paquito, my brother, and me, the eldest, lived in the basement. It was a majestic five-story property from the seventeenth century, prettiest thing I'd ever seen. But the place where we lived, oh God. It was a rusty room next to the central chimney. In the winter the smell of burnt firewood made it hard to breathe, and in the summer everything stank like sewage, the air tasted like rotten eggs. The room was so tiny we just had space for a small table we crowded around for every meal, and a full-size bed we all crammed into to sleep. We'd left home for the fanciest neighborhood in the world's most beautiful city, but we lived like war refugees."

Antonio's still holding my shoulder, his eyes filled with emotion, deep blue and misty, and I can see he genuinely thinks we are alike. I want to ask him if there's a cheerful ending to the story, ask him to tell me about that morning when he woke up with the smell of rotten eggs piercing his nose and yet Paris felt finally like home. I want him to say that every immigrant story about people who have been forced to abandon the place they thought they'd always belong ends that way, on a merry note, but nothing comes out of my mouth.

"We should get upstairs now," Catalina blurts out. "It's getting late, and I'm sure Belisario will wake up hungry any minute." She looks as moved as Antonio, wiping tears away with the back of her hand.

"Of c-course," Antonio stammers. He sounds apologetic. If he's blushing I can't tell, for his skin looks so red already.

We say our goodbyes and enter the lobby. When we reach the elevator, Zurbarán refuses to step in, pulling toward the stairs. He was supposed to be exhausted by now, but he wants to go out again, and the prospect of being in the apartment with Catalina while the baby sleeps fills me with anxiety. I step out of the elevator.

"Looks like he wants to walk a little more."

"His paws are a mess, Martín," she says. It's never good when she says my name. "He needs some rest."

"Agreed, but he seems to be thinking otherwise. I might just take him for a last quick stroll, and be back in no time."

Moaning sounds come from the stroller. Belisario stretches out his arms, then his legs. He's waking up.

"Whatever," she spits. "I just hope you know what you're doing, 'cause you're taking too many chances here, you understand? Too fucking many."

She pushes a button, and the doors slowly close. I try to think about the last time there wasn't tension between us, and it's hard to remember. Perhaps it was back when it was just the two of us, nothing, no one, else.

As Zurbarán and I walk west on the empty street, I imagine her alone in the empty apartment, feeding the baby, considering what to fix for lunch. I imagine her slitting open a bag of prewashed greens and tossing them with vinaigrette, while thinking about me, imagining me walking around the block with my sick dog and a smile on my face, thinking, What an asshole. What a horrible husband and pathetic father. How immature, how useless and cowardly. I imagine her asking herself why she's still with me and what's keeping her from leaving, from meeting someone else, a real man. Someone like my father.

We reach the corner of Gaztambide, and a white, stuccoed building rises in front of us. It has balconies on every floor, lush and full of green clay pots teeming with geranium blossoms so red they look swollen with blood. On the ground floor there's an adult day care center and, next to the entrance, a plaque on the wall that says Casa de las Flores. It explains that the building was built in the thirties, and almost destroyed in the Civil War. At some point during the war, it was home to Chilean poet Pablo Neruda.

I try to remember any of Neruda's poems, and I realize that the only thing I know about him is his name.

There's a bench outside, and I aim for it, feeling exhausted. It's so fucking hot. The buildings around me sizzle and pound.

Zurbarán coils into himself in the shade cast by the bench, and slides into a nap. He looks so old now, so eroded. I wish I could ease his pain and keep him alive. Dr. Ybarra suggested putting him to sleep. I couldn't do it. I want him to live for as long as possible. I don't want to be alone.

A white Lincoln Town Car flashes by and disappears around the corner, and I get goose bumps. It's the first time I've seen that type of car here. The last car my father had. It was the car he was driving the day he disappeared.

I check on Zurbarán. "You still there?" I whisper in his ears. "I wish I could love you more, or better," I say. His eyes remain closed.

I cover my mouth and sob like the orphan that I have become. I sob so hard I feel like my lungs are going to explode.

A few minutes later I hear the noise of tires screeching against pavement. I open my eyes, letting the daylight hurt me, and the Lincoln's parking in front of me, taking a spot designated for ambulances. The driver's door swings open, and Dad emerges from the car, giving me a wide, bright smile.

"So glad I came at this hour," he says mischievously as he approaches me, walking funny. "Jesus! It's so hard to find a parking spot in this city!"

He's wearing jeans and a sky-blue polo shirt; his salt-and-pepper hair is combed to perfection, shining brilliantly against the unrepentant sun. Zurbarán rises and starts to sniff around Dad's legs and the unusual sneakers he has on.

Dad looks athletic and relaxed, as if he'd finally caught up on the hours of sleep he'd been deprived of. He pets the dog, plays with his ears. Zurbarán reacts merrily and tries to lick his hands, but my father steps back.

He stands before me with his arms wide open, like a hawk gliding across the sky. I remain glued to the bench. I can't move.

"Aren't you going to give your father a hug?" Dimples in his cheeks. His presence is radiant and overpowering.

I look around the street; there's no one around.

"He's got my eyes," I say, pulling myself together, "and my nose and eyebrows and everything else, but the dimples are yours. I hadn't noticed before."

"So, no hug, huh?" Dad replies. He lowers his arms and scratches his neck a couple times, the gesture he does when something upsets him. He limps to the bench and takes a seat next to me. An electric shock runs down my spine. He breathes deeply and looks around, taking in the neighborhood. He stretches his arms and rests them on the back of the bench. I discreetly inch away, afraid that if he touches me I'll feel nothing.

"I understand if you don't want to hug me," he says. His eyes remain the same, but seem transparent now. They don't look tired or mad or sad. They're just on me, encompassing me. "We could try again later, right?"

His voice is exactly the same as before but calmer, as if he didn't have an opinion to impose this time around. He scans the street, then turns to me and smiles again. He smiles as if he weren't aware of what's happened to him, to us.

"You're so handsome, Son," he says. "Did I ever tell you that—"

"Your feet," I cut him off.

"Oh, yes," he says, taking a good look at the Puma sneakers he has on. They are apple-green with fluorescent yellow stripes and unbearably edgy. "What about them?"

"You have feet. Again, I mean."

"Yeah, well," he says. He bends forward and gives a quick brush to the sneakers with the tip of his fingers, looking uncomfortable. "These are, um, not really my feet, you know. I mean, look at those sneakers, look at the colors, the—"

"Whose feet are they?"

He clears his throat, and my stomach cramps for everything looks and feels so real, his voice, his gestures, his presence that always soothed me, regardless. "To be honest with you, I'm not sure. I got them at a flea market, and I preferred not to know all the details of the previous owner, if you know what I mean."

"They look too small for you."

"You're right!" He sounds relieved I'm not pressing further. "It feels funny, though, walking on them. Now I know what it was like for those poor Chinese girls, you know?"

"I miss you," I hear myself say out loud.

"I know," he says, and smiles again and goes silent, keeping his eyes on mine. "I miss you too. But you'll be fine. We'll all be fine, Son. I'm so proud of you."

"You could have told me that before," I say, and immediately regret having said it.

"You are a father now," he whispers. "You'll see for yourself that we, fathers, are full of shit."

"He's got my face. He's just like me. I'm terrified, Dad."

"I was terrified when you were born too. You'll be okay."

We talk for a while. He wants to know what it's like to live in Madrid. He wants to know if I'm planning to look for a job or open a business. He says a man should be busy, says that's the way a man earns his family's love and respect, and drops a couple of names of people in Spain who could help me.

He doesn't bring up the way he went missing, what happened to him, who did what to him, and I don't ask. I don't want to know. It's no use anymore.

Someone on one of the balconies above opens a window, and the sounds of a game show spoil the serenity. A siren howls in the distance. Madrid's coming back to life.

"Looks like someone might need the parking spot," Dad says. "I'd better get going; I don't want to run into trouble. Cops are hard to bribe around here, you know."

"I wish you'd stay longer."

"I do too," he says as he rises and tucks the polo shirt into his jeans. "But I have something else to tell you before I leave."

"What is it?"

"I know what's wrong with your dog."

I can't believe my ears.

"What's wrong with my dog, Dad?" I say, and can't help a smile.

"His feet."

"What's with them?"

"He's been barefoot all this time."

"He's a dog, Dad."

"I can't believe I never told you this."

"What about?"

"Dogs are not meant to be barefoot. Barefoot dogs always die young."

I don't know what to say. Dad squats down and pets Zurbarán, but he doesn't move. He remains asleep, enjoying himself in dreams.

"As long as you get him shoes, he'll be fine," he says, and rises again.

"The vet said he's got stomach cancer that has metastasized all over the place."

"Bullshit. He'll be fine."

I want to say I've no idea what he's talking about, but I don't want to disappoint him.

"Okay. I'll get him shoes," is all I say. "Thanks for the advice, Dad."

"Anytime, Son," he says, and reassures me with a look. "Okay. Gotta go now."

Dad opens his arms, and I rise, trembling. He's the one who approaches me. His body feels weightless, as if made of cork, the fabric of his polo eerie and crisp, and once we embrace I don't want to let him go, and I don't. We remain there, in the searing sun, thousands of miles away from home, until the aroma of roasted peanuts and mold that emanates from his skin evaporates, until he is gone.

# THE ARTEAGA FAMILY TREE

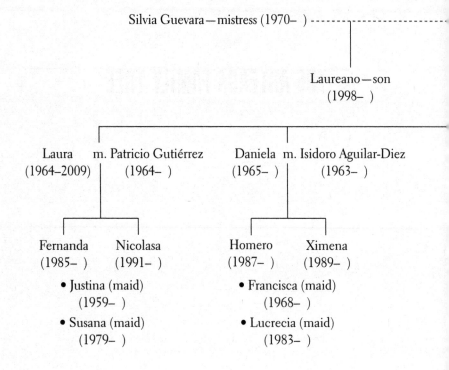

Silvia Guevara—mistress (1970– ) --------------------------

Laureano—son
(1998– )

Laura    m. Patricio Gutiérrez        Daniela   m. Isidoro Aguilar-Diez
(1964–2009)    (1964– )                (1965– )        (1963– )

Fernanda        Nicolasa           Homero          Ximena
(1985– )        (1991– )           (1987– )        (1989– )
• Justina (maid)                   • Francisca (maid)
  (1959– )                           (1968– )
• Susana (maid)                    • Lucrecia (maid)
  (1979– )                           (1983– )

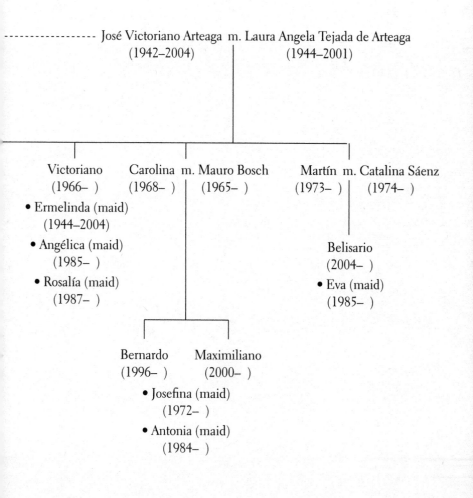

------------------ José Victoriano Arteaga m. Laura Angela Tejada de Arteaga
(1942–2004) (1944–2001)

Victoriano
(1966– )
• Ermelinda (maid)
(1944–2004)
• Angélica (maid)
(1985– )
• Rosalía (maid)
(1987– )

Carolina m. Mauro Bosch
(1968– ) (1965– )

Martín m. Catalina Sáenz
(1973– ) (1974– )

Belisario
(2004– )
• Eva (maid)
(1985– )

Bernardo Maximiliano
(1996– ) (2000– )
• Josefina (maid)
(1972– )
• Antonia (maid)
(1984– )

# ACKNOWLEDGMENTS

So many people have supported, encouraged, and advised me for the last eight years the list is ridiculously long. If I expressed in detail the reasons for my gratitude to all of them this section would be longer than the book itself, so I'll be brief.

Maria Hummel welcomed me into this language and encouraged me to make it my own. She was the first one to believe I could pull this off.

Oscar Cásares and Elizabeth McCracken embraced my work and advocated tirelessly for me—and still do. Elizabeth guided me wisely as I wrote the first draft, and keeps accepting my hugs in exchange. Oscar gifted me with his friendship and mentorship, and never misses lunch at Madam Mam's.

Edward Carey got excited by these stories and made me believe in them.

Dawn Garcia made the phone call that changed my life. She and Jim Bettinger at the Knight Fellowships made my dream come true. Ana Cristina Enríquez and Gabo Rodríguez-Nava helped me get there—here. This is basically their fault.

Sammie Sachs, Cecilia Yang, Jaslyn Law, Geri Smith, Erika Harrell, Katie Turner, Becca Tisdale, Nicole Chorney, Annika Ozinskas, Mia Arreola, Katherine Bell, Michelle Odemwingie, Chelsea Young, and Lisa Ruskin read my first pieces in English, and encouraged me to keep going. Without their early cheering I'd have given up.

Janine Zacharia and Dionne Bunsha patiently revised my early broken sentences, and never stopped rooting for me, have never stopped making me laugh.

Michael Collier at Bread Loaf gave me my first writing opportunity. Wayne Lesser nominated me for a fellowship at UT. John Pipkin awarded my thesis an award. Rebeca Romero supported me as my boss for four years, and shared countless screenshots for laughs.

Adam Johnson, Tom Kealey, Ted Conover, Jane Brox, Pete LaSalle, Thomas Cable, Jim Magnuson, Don Graham, Lisa Moore, Stephen Harrigan, Jake Silverstein, and Brigit Pegeen Kelly taught me how to do this. Noreen Cargill, Amy Stewart, Patricia Schaub, Marla Akin, Gwen Barton, and Melissa Kahn have made everything easier.

Cecily Sailer at Badgerdog gave me my first chance as a teacher. Carmen Johnson and Paul Lisicky said yes when everybody else was saying no. Honor Jones, Clay Smith, and Michael Bourne generously opened to me the doors to their publications.

Michael Adams made me cry over the phone. He and Dorothea took care of my family and me, and have gifted us with their friendship. The Graduate School at UT and the Texas Institute of Letters awarded me the Dobie Paisano Fellowship that allowed me to finish this book and convinced me that risks are worth taking.

Richard Abate took a leap of faith on the unpublished guy, and made the impossible happen.

Stefan Merrill Block proved that nothing moves without the generosity of noble strangers. This book would remain a manuscript without his excitement about it.

Nan Graham believed in the writer no one had heard

about and advocated for him since day one. Thanks to her, Scribner became my home—what else can I say? Can you believe it? I still can't.

Liese Mayer, my incredibly genius and generous editor, brought the Arteagas to life. Her tireless enthusiasm and intelligence turned a flawed draft into what you just read. This book would be way smaller without her caring wisdom.

Alex Merto, Mia Crowley-Hald, Erich Hobbing, and Kyle Kabel helped to produce a beautiful-looking book, and Kyle Radler helped to shout out from the rooftops.

Heera Kang, Lindsey Campion, Corinne Greiner, Kendra Fortmeyer, Ryan Bender-Murphy, Fiona McFarlane, Mary Miller, Greg Marshall, Monica Macansantos, Jeff Bruemmer, Ben Healy, Kate Finlinson, Taylor Flory Ogletree, Corey Miller, Carolina Ebeid, Virginia Reeves, Ben Roberts, and all of my other fellow writers at UT, Buddy Macatee, Liz Cullingford, Nina McConigley, Luis Alberto Urrea, Kevin McIlvoy, Matt Mendez, Myronn Hardy, Mike Scalise, Annita Sawyer, Kim Dana Kupperman, Eduardo Corral, Tomás Morín, Ben Fountain, Cristina Henríquez, Alfredo Corchado, Sarah Bird, Tom Zigal, Mary Helen Specht, Tyler Stoddard Smith, Francisco Goldman, Steph Opitz, Mark Doty, Elizabeth Gollan, Cecilia Ballí, Juan Pablo Villalobos, Daniel Alarcón, Carolina Guerrero, Laura Martínez, Sharan Saikumar, Elena Vega, Loren Corona, Javier Garza, Pam Naples, Edward Schumacher-Matos, Mark Stacey, Jorge Luis Sierra, Gabo Sama, Mara Behrens, Chucho del Toro, Lolbé Corona, Ana Paula Ayangui, Rocío Mino, Orieta Barbetta, José Antonio Herrera, Aidee Salinas, Lorena Flores, Samuel Belilty, Mike Gaytán, Jesus Chavez, Luis Patiño and everybody else at KAKW, Joel Salcido, Susana Guzmán, Aarón Sánchez, John Miguel and the Calverts, Marcia Brayboy, Nancy Rushefsky,

## ACKNOWLEDGMENTS

Bonnie Lister, Maarit and Sami Laurinen, Joao Andrade, Eric Thuau, Concha Fuente, Julià Monsó, Cristina Marzá, Dinorah, Fabiola, Mónica and Ofelia Rojas, Cata Laborde, Mariana Ortiz, Javier Pérez-Ilzarbe, Christel Peyrelongue, Federico Ortiz, Pedro Ortiz, Griselda Ruiz, Enrique Ruiz, tía Flor, tío Jorge, and Jorgito have all said words that kept me going.

Carlitos Gutiérrez has always been there, from Santa Fe through St. Mark's Place.

Neto Corona remains the brother I always wanted to have, decades strong.

My mom has been my mom, all along.

Emiliano and Guillermo have written the best part of my story, hands down. Life was so lame before you guys arrived.

And in the beginning, and in the end of everything I am, is, was, and will always be, Valentina. My first and last reader, my mantra, my home. The most beautiful Madrileña you'll ever find, the chatty girl from Montevideo who saved my life.